C·R·A·Z·Y
W·A·T·E·R

ELMER HOLMES BOBST AWARDS FOR EMERGING WRITERS

Established in 1983, the Elmer Holmes Bobst Awards in Arts and Letters are presented each year to individuals who have brought true distinction to the American literary scene. Recipients of the Awards include writers as varied as Toni Morrison, John Updike, Russell Baker, Eudora Welty, Edward Albee, Arthur Miller, Joyce Carol Oates, and James Merrill. The Awards were recently expanded to include categories devoted to emerging writers of fiction and poetry, and in 1995, the jurors selected winners in each category, Lori Baker for her short stories, *Crazy Water: Six Fictions*, Don Judson for his novella, *Bird-Self Accumulated*, and Debra Weinstein for her collection of poems, *Rodent Angel.*

C·R·A·Z·Y
W·A·T·E·R

SIX FICTIONS

Lori Baker

New York University Press
New York and London

NEW YORK UNIVERSITY PRESS
New York and London

Library of Congress Catologing-in-Publication Data
Baker, Lori
Crazy water : six fictions / Lori Baker.
p.   cm.
ISBN 0-8147-1283-5 (cloth : alk. paper). —ISBN 0-8147-1284-3
(pbk. : alk. paper)
I. Title.
PS3552.A43148C73   1996   95-50172
813.54—dc20   CIP

New York University Press books are printed on acid-free paper,
and their binding materials are chosen for strength and
durability.

for

PETER

• • •

CONTENTS

• • •

ACKNOWLEDGMENTS

"The Drive" previously appeared, in a somewhat different version, in the *Boston Review* (January 1987); "Romulus" appeared in *Cathay* (vol. 1, spring 1992) and in *Scraps* (Paradigm Press, 1995).

C·R·A·Z·Y
W·A·T·E·R

• • •

Grace

1. Definitions

My good friend Grace grew up in a shadowy house on a suburban street as clean and brilliant and shadowless as a razor blade. On most afternoons, Grace in her pink dress was the only ellipse in a Mondrian of perfectly planed white fences advancing to curbs stiffer than hospital beds and hedges marching like evergreen soldiers around carefully researched borders. Although she might have held a ball or a jump rope or a plastic truck, play was a mystery to Grace, for she was dedicated to the sanctity of her dress. Wrinkles and dirt were forbidden, and Mother, peering out of the back window from behind an ingenuously draped curtain, made certain it was so.

Grace's house was full of shadows, although it was just as big, and white, and wide windowed as the houses all around it. The shadows emanated not from some architectural blunder but from Grace's mother, who was a woman of complex moods and mysterious disappointments. Every day when Mother stepped out to the curb to get the mail she stood for a moment, looking up and down the street with its identical houses, and imagined other women, identical to herself, stepping out to identical mailboxes to fetch identical mail (the telephone bill, the electric bill, some flyer advertising rump roast at thirty-five cents a pound).

Coming back into the house and looking at Grace, she'd say, "More of the same, more of the same, more of the same," over and over like a prayer. Grace pondered her words, as if they contained some lesson, some key.

When she was pregnant, Mother said, she had had a dream in which she saw herself at the seashore, playing in the water with a golden child of exquisite beauty. Then she had gone to the hospital, she said, "and you came out." Grace was not an exquisite golden child; she was small and dark and vaguely funny looking, and as she grew she was followed everywhere by the vast shadow of her mother's disapproval. Every day the shadow followed her down the street and all the way to school. Only there, once she had slipped beneath the principal's arm and through the dingy green entrance doors, did the shadow recede, allowing Grace to bounce a ball and put wrinkles into her dress.

"You mark my words," Mother would say, scowling at the wrinkles when Grace returned home from school promptly at three fifteen, "no one will ever want you, if you don't learn how to keep yourself up."

Grace of course had no idea who might want her, or for what, and when she asked, her mother's face took on a strange and righteous stiffness, as if Grace had just confirmed or perhaps rather satisfied her gravest suspicions. "Never mind for what, just keep your dress straight," Mother cryptically replied.

So Grace stood stiffly on the back lawn holding her ball, a tiny ellipse in a field of rectangles.

Grace took Mother very seriously. Then as now, what my friend lacked in beauty, she made up for in earnestness. For days she pondered her mother's mysterious oracular fables, just as, years later, she would ponder with the same fierce trustingness statements made by hocus pocus gypsies over her passively proffered palm ("ten dollars per hand, or twenty dollars for a Tarot reading, dear"). Whatever conclusions she drew, she kept them to herself and tried harder not to wrinkle her dress.

One afternoon, Grace returned home from school in need of a definition. A strange and mysterious word had grown up like mildew on the salmon-tiled wall of a small room called Girls somewhere on Corridor 3. The word, which had begun, like mildew, faintly, had become darker and darker as the week went on, until it was so engorged by the humid squirmy giggles of a dozen prepubescent females that it began to loom in Grace's young mind like a lichen-covered bat or a cave—emanating fetid poisonous gases. They all knew what it meant; Grace didn't.

"Fuck," Mother said, without lifting up her dust rag, "means something very dirty that has to do with girls."

Aha. Grace stored the definition away in her mind for later reference and went into the kitchen to get a cookie. After all, she was only eight.

"If you have to eat that, make sure you don't get crumbs on my rug," Mother said. "No one will look at you twice, Grace, if you can't keep a house clean."

And what about Father? Where was he while all this was going on?

"Probably out with that woman, that blond of his," Mother said, adjusting her vacuum cleaner to the setting for deep pile carpet.

At least, that's what Grace told me.

Grace

2. Shells

When she was in junior high school, Grace began collecting seashells. Their names were magic incantations, whispered under cover of darkness in her clean white bedroom: sundial and lion's paw, bleeding tooth and angel's wing, moon snail and shark eye, dogwinkle and whelk. Sitting alone in her very neat bedroom, Grace could stare for hours at the pink-lipped curve of a cowry or a conch, as if she might find the secrets of eternity in those smooth shining folds. The inanimate glistening whorls of the sea dead had become easier for her to penetrate than the complex, spiraling adolescent minds that surrounded her every day at school. Somehow, over the course of a single summer spent completing paint-by-numbers in the back yard, Grace had become lost. Afloat on a raft of anxiety, she found herself propelled through the teeming hallways of the junior high school by convulsive waves of hormone and angst that she couldn't comprehend.

Foremost among the dreads was her math teacher, Mr. Evangeline. His flat fishy eyes, regarding Grace cryptically through thick, opalescent lenses, set her repeating a seashell mantra as she huddled at her desk. Every day she sailed further away from polynomials and graph paper, shutting herself for protection inside the flame of a sunset scallop or a bristling murex. Nothing Evangeline said could convert Grace to a belief in the reality of mathematics; worse yet, she was terrified by the bristling wart that protruded from his pale damp cheek, just beneath the steel ridge of his glasses. Every now and then he would wake her from some briny daydream by slapping an exam paper down on her desk. The exams that startled her so on their arrival inevitably returned to her a few days later bearing grades like D or F.

Good, clean, quiet, obedient, perfectly ironed Grace was flunking mathematics, and she was amazed.

What amazed her most of all was that flunking required no will. Somehow Grace had always thought that failure involved a concerted non-effort, a decision to cut loose and float freely through and above and beyond those glowing inscrutable diatoms that Mr. Evangeline called formulae. Instead it was just the opposite. She did not intend to flunk, but she flunked anyway, and she flunked everything: homework, quizzes, midterms, even class participation.

Her mother was furious.

"People who are really intelligent are intelligent at *everything*," Mother said, bristling with innuendo.

Mother found Grace's failure unendurable. After

all, if Grace insisted on being small and dark and funny looking, she could at least be smart.

There was a flurry of visits to the math department: Mother insisted that Mr. Evangeline change Grace's grade. New information was revealed: Grace was lazy. She didn't listen, she daydreamed in class. If she had listened, she would have passed. One day she had dropped a book on the floor; she'd been reading *it* instead of the math book. Grace didn't get along with the other children; it seemed to him, Mr. Evangeline said, that she was *afraid*, and so she didn't speak up in class. If only she had bothered to ask questions, she would have passed.

In short, it was Grace's fault, and her grade for the term would remain an F.

Still, there was hope for next term. Mother hired Mr. Evangeline to tutor Grace in math, at twenty dollars an hour, flat rate.

The idea that sly, damp-smiling Mr. Evangeline should enter her own home horrified Grace. How could she sit in that kitchen chair again, once Mr. Evangeline had rested there? How could she touch the kitchen table? Ever again drink out of a water glass, once he'd sipped? All of home would be contaminated, once Mr. Evangeline arrived with his briefcase and his evasive mathematical eyes.

Grace squirmed; she shouted; she begged.

Mother was inexorable. She said that Mr. Evangeline would come; and he came.

From her frilly-curtained bedroom window, Grace watched him come. He had on his long brown coat buttoned up tight around his neck; from her vantage point she could see dull patches of wear on the shoulders. He didn't have his briefcase, but something was tucked beneath his arm. It looked ominously like a math book.

Mr. Evangeline tiptoed delicately up the walk, trying to evade patches of sharp glinting February ice, and perhaps, instinctively, Grace's poisonous glances. A plume of frosty breath emerged from his mouth and encircled his balding, hatless head.

"Grace," Mother called from downstairs. "GraACE! Mr. Evangeline's here!"

Grace clenched a seashell in her hand and said nothing.

"Grace!" Mother called again, with a warning in her voice.

"Just a minute, Mother," Grace shouted down, but sweetly. "I'm in the bathroom. Just a minute!"

It was the first lie that Grace had ever told, and she had told it to her mother. And it worked. Mother stopped calling, and Grace heard a dull raspy mumbling, like stones being turned over by the tide.

Grace

Her mother was talking to Mr. Evangeline.

My friend, who had never in her life known a moment of duplicity, was struck by a sudden longing to hear what they were saying. Later on, she would remember that moment, when she snuck barefoot down her mother's immaculately carpeted stairs, seashell in hand, as a sort of unveiling.

"Eve bit the apple," she told me, much later.

Good, clean, quiet, obedient, slightly wrinkled Grace knelt on the dining room floor next to her Mother's china cabinet, pressed her ear against the door, and listened.

The first thing she heard was the humid "har-ummph" of Mr. Evangeline clearing his throat, perhaps in preface to some incomprehensible mathematical statement.

"Well, my feeling," Mr. Evangeline was saying, "is that some kids just don't have the ability. You can push and push, Ma'am, but if she hasn't got it she hasn't got it, and no amount of pushing will give it to her, if you know what I mean."

"So then you agree," Mother said, "that she just isn't as bright as the nice *normal* children. I told my husband. I told him last year's grades were just a fluke."

"Well, now, *normal* . . . ," Mr. Evangeline began.

"You know, Mr. Evangeline," Grace heard Mother say, in a very confidential tone, "Grace has never really been what I'd call *normal*. She's just not like other children, Mr. Evangeline, she's not. You've hit it right on the head."

Grace imagined her mother leaning forward in her blond wood kitchen chair.

"I would give everything," Mother said, "if only my child could be normal, like the others."

"Well Ma'am," Mr. Evangeline said, "we'll do the best we can, won't we?"

As Grace sat with her red adolescent ear pressed to the dining room door, Mother continued to talk. She talked all about Grace: superstitiously about Grace's birth ("I knew right away something was wrong—they said she was up there backwards!"); about Grace's toddlerhood ("She refused to suck her thumb. Can you imagine a child refusing to suck her thumb? We had to put it in her mouth for her!"); about Grace's elementary school years ("Too precocious—the questions she asked me!").

And Mr. Evangeline talked. He talked all about Grace: scornfully about Grace's ineptitude in mathematics ("I was quite amazed by her faulty grasp of negative numbers, Ma'am"); about Grace's shyness ("She sits there like a scared little animal—scared of those kids, Ma'am, I just don't understand it"); about Grace's poor work habits ("Every page covered with erasures, some so bad they tore right through the paper!").

Sitting there behind the dining room door, Grace turned the conch shell over in her hands, and wished that she could slip between its pink protective lips, down and away into an enameled vault where mathematics and mothers and Mr. Evangeline didn't reach.

And so she did.

As she sat there on the dining room floor (hard wood polished until it gleamed), my friend Grace climbed inside her conch shell. She slid on the satiny pink and white interior into a labyrinth of swoops and curves and dizzying spirals, through rooms huge and small, passages sinister and smiling, all of it glowing softly like the sea. She could hear the sea: the sound of waves was all around her, very nearly drowning out Mr. Evangeline's nasal pronouncement:

"You can't make 'em what they aren't, Ma'am!"

So Grace slid farther; she slid deeper and deeper into the shell; she slid toward the sea. She slid until she was surrounded by the ocean. Fronds of seaweed caressed her knees. A yellow and blue filefish (*Oxymonacanthus longirostris,* so she'd read in *Fishes of the*

Barrier Reef, so rudely torn from her grasp) grazed in her long dark hair. In place of her mother's voice Grace heard . . . nothing.

The silence was resounding, aquatic, multidimensional. Tucked away in her seashell far below the waves, Grace had finally escaped from her mother.

But the dining room door rocked open, and there, from very far away, Grace saw her mother standing above her, hands on hips, smiling cunningly.

"There you are, dear! All set to do some math?" Mother asked.

Mother's voice was very faint. She couldn't see that Grace, safe inside her shell, was in a place that mathematics would never reach.

Grace smiled politely, and hoped there was no seaweed in her teeth.

"Yes, Mother," she said.

3. Rights of Trespass

When she was seventeen, in the autumn, my friend Grace fell in love for the very first time. It was an extraordinary fall—the maple trees were already shot through with scarlet when it happened; Grace had started wearing her thick black hair tied back in a bun. Over the summer, she had learned to rule perfect margins around her essays—one inch all around, except for two inches, at the top, where the titles were written in.

"The titles were the surprise," she said.

And so they were. Grace wrote the papers at night; she wrote the titles in the morning, before breakfast.

At seventeen Grace spent most evenings in her mother's dark kitchen, pressing her dress with an iron. In the morning, she wore the dress on the schoolbus, where other girls (with pink angora sweaters, and shiny metal braces, and perfume that smelled, just faintly, of bubblegum) conjectured about her age: seventeen, or forty? It happened four times every day: when Grace got on the bus and when she got off, going to school and going home.

At seventeen Grace had ceased entirely to be like other girls. The angora sweaters passed by her like a dream. Seventeen, or forty? They snapped their gum, flipped their cigarette butts at her feet. She sat primly in her green vinyl seat, clutching her books to her chest, waiting for everybody else to file off the bus. Grace was always the last one off the bus in the morning; she was the last one on the bus in the afternoon.

Grace had finally learned how to fit into her

mother's neatly ordered world: she made herself entirely out of straight lines, so that when she walked past the white fences and surly hedgerows and stiff inexorable sidewalks of her neighborhood, she too was stiff, straight, and inexorable. Her dress was always perfectly pressed; her notebooks were always perfectly neat; her margins were always perfectly ruled; her hair was always drawn straight back to the perfectly inflexible white nape of her seventeen year old neck. That knot of black hair, resting at the nape of her neck, was the only thing about her that wasn't straight—that and the slight swelling of the tiny breasts that huddled like shy refugees behind her perfectly ironed dress front. If those slight swellings suggested something soft, something vulnerable, something less than architectural in Grace's ensemble, no one bothered to notice; Grace always walked with her books clutched against them, just in case.

Grace had learned how to fit into the *interior* of her Mother's world, as well. Inside the house, Grace did chores. She did chores in the morning; she did chores after school. When she wasn't doing chores, Grace did her homework. She sat at the white desk in her bedroom, and concentrated very hard, conjugating the verb *to be* in Spanish: *soy, eres, es; somos, sois, son.* Every now and then Grace's mother peeked inside, to make sure Grace was still working. Grace's pen was always at the paper: *Yo soy una chica Americana*, she wrote. *Yo quiero . . .*

I want something, but what?

Something more . . .

On occasion, Grace's mother went away. Grace's father had been gone by then, for a very long time, and that meant that Grace's mother, who preferred to stay inside the house, sometimes had to go out. Grace's mother sometimes walked down Main Street to the supermarket; she pushed an empty shopping cart in front of her all the way down Main Street, even past the point where the sidewalk ended, and the traffic came very close to the edges of the pavement and very close, by extension, to the hem of Mother's sundress. Later, she pushed the shopping cart, full, all the way back home.

The walk to the supermarket was fraught with danger; that's what Grace's mother said.

"I almost died today," she sometimes intoned, as she stood in the kitchen, unloading groceries into her perfectly cleaned, perfectly polished, perfectly organized blond wood cabinets.

Once, as Grace's mother pushed her shopping cart to the market, she came right up to a thick black snake that had slithered onto the road. She said it was a water moccasin; she said that if she had taken another step, she would have died.

"I almost died," Mother said, "and then what would you have done? What would have happened to you then, Grace?"

Grace only shrugged her very straight, very slender shoulders. What would Grace do without Mother? *Yo soy una chica Americana*, she thought, rehearsing. *Yo quiero . . .*

Grace helped her mother put away the groceries, but she didn't walk with her to the supermarket. Grace's job on marketing day was to stay at home and do her homework. Mother always wanted Grace to get an A on her marketing day homework.

"After all," Mother would say, "you had the whole house to yourself. Nice and quiet, while I walked to the market to get food for you."

At seventeen, Grace had learned how to satisfy her mother. She almost always got an A, or something like it. An A−. Or, if it were mathematics, a B+. Mother was happy. Grace was happy.

Shopping day was Grace's favorite day. She liked to stand at the front window, and watch as Mother went down the driveway with her shopping cart, wearing her sundress and a big straw hat. As the days shortened into fall, the sundress was topped with a sweater; then it was exchanged for a heavier dress, and an old jacket of Father's—sort of a rain jacket, with a zip up the front. Grace watched as Mother disappeared around the corner, behind a fence and a big mulberry hedge.

Grace always waited until Mother was very much out of sight. Then—instead of going upstairs, and sitting at her white desk, and doing her homework, as Mother must have imagined—Grace went outside, into the thick stand of evergreen trees that bordered her mother's back yard, and smoked a cigarette.

My friend was so good in those days, so very straight, so very pressed and neat and efficiency cornered, that no one could have imagined that cigarette: not her mother, not the girls on the school bus, not the teachers who admired her expertly kept margins, not even her own father, who was long since launched on secretive misdeeds of his own. No one could have imagined Grace, perched sidesaddle on a low branch of one of those evergreens—encased in the silence and the slightly bitter scent of the trees that she had called (as a child lacking all sense of proportion and perspective) "the Woods"—expertly inhaling from her cigarette and gazing up among the tangled branches. There were patches of sunlight up there, struggling through the thick nubbles of green; occasionally a bluejay or a blackbird flitted over her head, and then the branches swayed, dropping pine needles into her hair.

Grace, who had become an expert at hiding

things inside herself, had also become an expert at hiding things outside herself—like a pack of cigarettes inside a hollow tree; and at hiding *herself*, here among the evergreens.

When she exhaled, the smoke rose up through the branches, and disappeared, like a secret, into the blue autumnal sky.

As a child, Grace had played among these trees, when her mother would let her—or on those rare occasions when her mother wasn't looking. For hours, Grace could sit among the branches, while her mother tried calling her to dinner from various windows of their big suburban house. The ground was covered with pine needles, dried to a sharp, pungent brown; Grace loved to scrape them aside until she reached the rich black soil underneath, redolent of earthworms and tiny white mushrooms. Grace loved the smell of it, the feel of it: a world beneath the surface, complete, invisible, mysterious, protected by the thorny forbidding layer of pine needles that lay above it.

"It was a lot," she told me later, "like I thought love must be."

Hidden. Secret. Far away from Mother's prying eyes.

Not that Grace intentionally set out to deceive

her mother. It was simply very pleasant, crouching there among the trees, inhaling from her cigarette as she had once inhaled, with pleasure, the sweet black-smelling earth beneath the pine needles. Nothing was straight there, or neat there, or very orderly; everything was tangles, webs, confusions: branches broken, branches crooked, branches fighting, just like Grace, toward the sun.

And love was there, huddled among the branches. It was there long before Grace saw it, long before Grace was ready to see it. But one day Grace was ready; and on that day, the second shopping day in October, as Grace sat on her branch in her well-ironed dress, smoking her cigarette and being careful not to get pine sap on her sleeves, she looked up into the trees, and saw love.

There was nothing prepossessing about it, at first sight. At first Grace wasn't sure that she had seen it at all. Something caught her eye—a glint, or a sparkle, up there in the pine—and she had to stare very hard, and very long, up into the deep green fronds, in order to discover it again. The sky that day was very blue and clear; it glinted through the branches like a hail of brittle autumnal sapphires and made it very hard for Grace to see. But nonetheless, there it was: a dark lump wadded into one of the many triangles

formed by trunk and branch, and at its midst, something that glittered, something that had caught
Grace's eye. Something shiny, up there in a tree.

From where she sat, with her cigarette between
her fingers, Grace couldn't tell what it was. She
didn't know that it was love. She only knew that
there was something up there, stuck in her favorite
tree.

Something that didn't belong.

Whatever it was, it bothered the Grace who was
neat and straight and orderly—the Grace who had
learned to rule perfect margins around her essays
(one inch all around, except for two inches, at the top,
where the titles were written in). Whatever it was,
Grace was going to get rid of it.

So she stubbed out her cigarette, and slipped off
her shoes, and then good, clean, quiet, obedient Grace
mounted the lowest branch, and began to climb up
her favorite tree.

What did Grace think while she climbed? Not
much about love, huddled in the branches above her.
Instead she thought about her perfectly ironed dress,
and how she would have to hide it, or maybe even
throw it away, so that Mother wouldn't see the
smears of pitch on the pockets, or the bits of bark and
pine sticking to the hem.

Good, clean, quiet, obedient Grace.

Grace

She had other thoughts, too; that's what she told me later. She told me that when she was a child, hiding in the Woods with the sparrows around her ears, she had dreamed of finding gemstones lodged among the tree trunks. Diamonds and rubies and emeralds and opals, stuck away between the toes of the trees.

Grace thought about them again, as she climbed in her bare feet to the spot where love was glittering between the branches.

Finally, she reached it. Grace balanced on a slender branch, face to face with love, terrified of falling. It was all she could do to reach out, plunge her hand into the soft dark bundle, and tuck it up under her armpit. For a split second, she looked out through a gap in the pine cover into the blue sky, and down over the yard: there was the swingset, and the clothesline, and the big aloof back of her mother's house, all looking very small. Then, trembling, Grace felt her way back down the tree.

Back on the ground, Grace took the dark bundle out from under her arm. She saw that she was holding clothing: a dark cotton shirt (brown and grey, like the underside of a sparrow) with buttons at the collar and the cuffs, somebody's sap-stained trousers, and a pair of glossy men's shoes, with socks stuffed into the toes, and, tied around it all, a necktie.

It was the zipper that had caught her eye, glinting in the hard October sun.

Grace spread the clothes out over a branch; she lit a new cigarette; she inhaled deeply, and watched the smoke vanish into the treetops. Quietly, Grace contemplated the clothes. She thought that they were a man's clothes. She thought that since she hadn't seen them in the tree yesterday, they had been put in the tree today. She thought that perhaps somebody would be returning later to claim them. She thought that she would like to see who.

Good, clean, quiet, obedient Grace rolled the clothes up into a bundle, and decided to take them away.

"That way," she told me, "he had to come to *me* to get them back."

Grace put the clothes under a tree. Then she went into her mother's big clean house and got her warm jacket; she took two pieces of paper out of a drawer; on one she wrote her mother a note.

"Mother," Grace wrote, in her perfect cursive.

"Gone to the library to work on my science project. Will be back later. Love, Grace."

It was the second lie that Grace had ever told her mother, and although she wouldn't admit it, I suspect that she thought, as she wrote it, about how well the first lie had worked.

Grace

Grace's mother would be displeased, perhaps even angry. And thinking about her mother's anger, Grace remembered to go into her room and take her science book and her science notebook, so that her lie would look more convincing, later, when she came home from the library.

Then Grace went back out into the Woods, with her jacket and her science books, and she wrote another note. Calmly, in a straight, neat, firm hand, she printed out the words: "NO TRESPASSING." She didn't really think, as she wrote the note, about who might read it; she didn't think, as she secured it up in the branches of the pine with a bobby pin from her own well-organized hair, what the reaction to her note might be. And then she sat in the pine needles, and waited.

She said she waited calmly, but I'll bet that she was anxious. After all, it was October, and it was evening; it was getting dark, and my friend was clutching a stranger's clothes in her lap. The clothes smelled faintly of smoke, and of something else, something that Grace had never smelled before but that she knew must be the smell of a man's skin, clinging to his clothes. As the sun began to sink and it grew dark between the pines, Grace hugged the clothes against her chest and inhaled the unfamiliar scent and felt a little warmer.

Her mother would have been horrified.

But her mother didn't know. As she sat among the trees, Grace had heard her mother come home—heard her mother's footsteps on the porch, and the snap of the back door slamming as she carried in the groceries. Grace's mother would have read the note; and while Grace was outside, growing a little stiff from the cold and damp, her mother would think that she was at the library, working on her science project.

The sun fell, and soon it was completely dark among the pines. It was quiet, too, except for rustling noises in the treetops, and the very distant *swish* of the cars passing on Main Street. Grace imagined squirrels in the trees, and middle-aged businessmen in the cars, heading home to families, and pickles, and plates of hot roast beef. She imagined her mother, turning on the lights in the living room. Every night, precisely at fifteen minutes after sunset, Mother turned on the lights; every night, precisely at fifteen minutes after eleven, she turned them off, when she and Grace went to bed.

Grace thought a little bit about her dress for the next day, and how she wouldn't have time to press it, and how she would look wrinkled, when she got onto the school bus.

And then she heard, very distinctly, stealthy footsteps crunching through the leaves at the side of her mother's house. Good, clean, quiet, obedient Grace huddled down among the trees with the clothes against her chest, and heard the footsteps come closer; she heard the parting of the pine branches, and saw the tiny glowing knob of his cigarette pass just above her head. She heard the pine branches creak as he climbed—then the crackle of paper, and a voice, softly:

"Oh, shit!"

There was probably just enough left of the dwindling October light—at least, high up in the tree, where *he* was—to read Grace's note. It struck her as very funny, Grace told me later, that her silly note could cause such consternation. It was so funny, she said, that she might have laughed aloud—out of nervousness, of course.

There was silence up in the tree then, and silence down below it.

Then, a man's voice again:

"Who is that? I heard you laughing, y'know!"

She heard him slide back down through the tree and land, with a thud, on the pine-muffled earth. Much stumbling amid the branches; then:

"Dammit, give me my clothes!"

Grace laughed; a cigarette lighter flicked; there they were, eye to eye, only a few feet apart, with a thick pine bough between them. He was young—a year or two older than Grace, perhaps—with thick curly black hair, receding a little bit at the temples, and dark eyes.

"You've got my clothes," he said. He could see them. Grace still had them, clutched against her chest.

"Yes," she said.

"Well, hand 'em over!"

He held out his hand and the cigarette lighter went out, so that he was just a silhouette again.

"No," Grace said.

Many years later, Grace told me, she couldn't believe that she had said it. Good, clean, quiet—suddenly not-so-obedient Grace?

"Hey, they're mine," he said, and took a step toward her—a step that might have been threatening, except that he had forgotten the thick branch between them. "Listen, lady, you've got no right to keep my clothes!"

"I'm not a *lady*," Grace snapped, thinking about the girls on the bus, and their bubblegum perfume *(seventeen? or forty?)*. "I'm seventeen, and you've got no right to leave your clothes in my back yard!"

He was quiet then; Grace could hear him breathing.

"You're right," he said, voice ringing with false

contrition. "I'm very sorry. Now, will you give me back my clothes?"

Grace hugged the bundle of clothing tighter against her chest.

"Why?" she said.

"Why? Because they're mine and I need them, that's why."

"I mean," Grace said, carefully, "why did you leave them here? I mean," she continued, giggling a little (out of nervousness, of course), "don't you need to wear your clothes?"

He was wearing clothes, of course; she had seen in the snatch of lighter-light that he had on dirty-looking jeans, a flannel shirt, and sneakers.

"Listen," he said, suddenly humbled, "please give me the clothes. My old lady'll kill me if I come home like this."

All at once, Grace was interested; she might have been thinking about her own orderly mother, watching television in the big white house—and probably checking the clock, and wondering when Grace would be home.

The young man's voice dropped lower, became suddenly confidential. "She thinks I'm working," he said. "So I go out every day in those," he gestured toward the clothes Grace was holding, a little bit less tenaciously, in her lap, "and then I stop here, and I change into these, and off I go. Same thing at night, only in reverse."

He didn't say where he went, and Grace didn't ask. Something stirred in the branches above them, and pine needles tinkled past.

"All right," she said, and held out the soft bundle at arm's length. "You can have your clothes back."

He reached out and took the clothes. His fingers might have touched hers when he took them. If they had (and on this point my friend preserves a sphinxlike silence), it might have been the first time that a man's hand had touched hers.

Except for Father's hand of course: and that was different.

Once he took the clothes, though, he seemed to forget her—he seemed to assume that Grace had gone, melted back into the branches perhaps. He turned his back. My friend, who had always been so polite, found it very rude indeed: that broad back, turned away from her. As she watched, he pulled the flannel shirt up over his head; then, back still turned, he stepped out of his jeans and hung them on a tree. In the dark his pale skin glowed, indistinctly, like a ghost or a will-o'-the-wisp.

My friend Grace, crouched among the trees, tried

very hard to become invisible. She had succeeded before, many times; cowering before Mother or mathematics or the taunts of the children on the school bus, she could disappear inside herself until she became, most assuredly, transparent. But this time she couldn't; something held her back.

Many years later, she confided something that she could never have told her mother.

"I wanted to *look*," she said.

So she looked; and I think that she saw very little, there in the dark, in October, between the trees.

My friend was both tantalized and afraid, there among the damp roots of her childhood. What could she have been afraid of? Mother had never told her anything; Grace was perfectly, politely, innocent. Still, she was filled with a foreboding that the young man, in his ignorance, seemed unwilling to confirm; for he truly seemed to have forgotten her. He buttoned up his formal shirt and pulled on his trousers; he even put on his shoes, all without looking around even once. Within minutes he was transformed from a sylph to a businessman—except that his tie was left loose and hung free around his neck. Grace thought she could have met him at an office somewhere, or maybe he would be traveling door to door.

"How do you do, Ma'am," he'd say, and hand a

catalogue across the front stoop. Grace giggled, imagining herself in a housecoat and curlers, answering the door.

Then he turned around—he remembered that she was there.

"You watched," he said.

Grace stood up. She had her science books under her arm.

"Yes," she said. After all, what was the point of lying?

He came toward her then, around the tree, until he was standing very close. In the dark, she couldn't see the expression in his eyes. He touched her face.

"Do you like to watch?" he asked.

Then he kissed her. His lips felt hard and dry and awkward against hers; his whiskers scratched against her cheek. Grace gasped, stumbled backwards against a tree, turned around . . . and ran. She thought she heard him running behind her, imagined his hand reaching out for her dress, for her hair (the bun, which she had wound up so carefully just this morning, had fallen out, and now her hair was down around her shoulders, hairpins and all); but when she emerged from the Woods into the light at the back of her mother's big white house, no one was there. The thick line of pines was completely dark, completely silent. He hadn't chased her.

Grace

She'd been running from nothing.

Grace stooped among her mother's bushes to straighten her dress and retwist her hair. She saw that a single light was on in the living room, just like always. This evening, like every evening Grace could remember, Mother would be sitting on the couch, watching television; this evening, like every other, she would expect Grace to come inside quietly, set up the ironing board, and begin to press her clothes for the next day.

And Grace did go in; she went straight to the living room, with her science books cradled in her arms, to kiss her mother goodnight. But she didn't press any dresses; instead she went upstairs, and sat in the dark by the window, watching the Woods, and waiting. She waited until midnight, and when no one appeared, Grace knew that she must have missed him; that while she had been running back toward her mother's house, he had been running in the opposite direction. He had emerged onto Main Street, with his bundle of clothes; he had gone home.

Grace lay awake in the dark for a long time. When she finally slept, she dreamed, darkly, of kisses.

The next morning, and for all the mornings that would follow, Grace didn't twist up her hair. She pressed her dresses less and less: first every other evening, then every third evening, then hardly at all.

Her mother noticed something new about her: a sort of laxity, a softness, something unstarched; as if something that had been covered up for a very long time had finally come free.

• • •

The Drive

Where were they when it started? Nobody knows anymore, nobody cares. Elspeth and Sabina were fighting in the back seat, Pearl's shoulders in the paisley blouse were stiff and straight in the front seat, Daddy behind the steering wheel seemed unimportant to all of them, except that the smoke from his cigarette was giving Pearl a headache she thought she would never forgive him for. Lots of stuff was passing by outside the windows: crowded trees with blood-red tops and slim black trunks, clear crooning streams distilled through granite-pebbled banks, soft mountains with their tops buried moodily in cloud. But Elspeth and Sabina were fighting over a pink-backed mirror, and Pearl with the blossom of pain behind her ear stared without seeing anything. Maybe Daddy was listening to the wet ticking of the tires on the damp pavement.

They had already passed so many roadside stands

with handwritten signs that said Apples, Cider, Maple Syrup, that Daddy had stopped pointing them out.

Certain things are worth knowing: the twins, in the back seat, were desperate to take possession of the mirror, in spite of the fact that each one saw her reflection in the face of the other. Pearl, who wore the paisley blouse, was not their mother. She wished they had not come. When Daddy had stopped to pick them up at the home of his former wife, they had been sitting on the floor, drawing. How cute, how sweet, Daddy might have thought. This is what they had been drawing: pictures of Pearl, with tall green curlicue hair and a fat orange body made of ovoids that reminded Daddy of turds.

Daddy drove silently with the cigarette hanging from his mouth. His cheeks were covered with grey stubble.

Pearl's hair was not really green, but it was very tall. It did rise in blond curlicues toward the roof of the car.

Sabina and Elspeth wore *their* fine blond hair tied back from their faces in little pink bows, just like one worn by their mother that morning, when Daddy came to pick them up.

The car windows were dirty. All the stuff passing by outside looked duller because of that. And in fact the sky was grey. The clouds were very low; that was why no one in the car could have seen the mountains, if they had cared to look.

But they could, if they had cared to roll down the windows, have breathed in with dark foreboding the scent of deep forest, rotting leaves, cold water over stone.

Instead they breathed the smoke from Daddy's cigarette.

The car was rolling over a damp stretch of road, deserted. Wet leaves stuck to the tires, so that they seemed to tick.

Eventually, Pearl began to talk. She talked about her headache. She talked about the twins. "Jesus Christ," said Pearl, "if you can't control your own children. You have to start somewhere, controlling something, instead of making *me* suffer, as always *I'm* the one who gets the headache, it's never *you*, now, is it? Is it?"

Pearl pressed her hand, with its flamingo pink fingernails, to the back of her neck.

"You're right, of course, Pearl," said Daddy, listlessly.

Maybe that was when it started. Maybe it had already started then, although Daddy didn't tell them.

Sabina and Elspeth stopped fighting in the back

seat to listen to Pearl talk. If they had had pieces of paper, they would have drawn her like this: three barking heads emerging from the collar of the paisley blouse, a fat round body culminating in hooves rather than feet. She might have had a tail, too.

Pearl was still talking. "Naturally, I have to come up with *all* the ideas. If not for me we would sit at home in the living room *all* the time. And then what do you do?"

Elspeth poked her head over the front seat. "Daddy," she said.

Daddy ignored her, although Pearl stopped talking suddenly, with her mouth still open.

"Daddy," Elspeth insisted, "I have to *piss*."

"My *God*," said Pearl, throwing up her hands. "Do you see what I mean? *Do you see what I mean?*"

Daddy didn't look away from the road. "Simmer down, now," he said.

"Daddy!"

"Elspeth, honey, I heard you," Daddy sighed.

He sighed because the road laughed wetly ahead, up and down hills, without any sign of a rest area or a roadside stand. Only trees that crowded close to the pavement.

For awhile, everyone sat in silence, except for Elspeth. She bounced around in the back seat, crossing and uncrossing her legs in their white tights.

The Drive

Sabina gazed at her reflection in the pink-backed mirror, looking sometimes at her twin, as if for reference.

"My God," groaned Pearl. "To think that this was all my idea. To think that I let myself in for this!" She delicately patted her curlicue hair.

"Now, Pearl," said Daddy.

"Oh no! No, no, no," Pearl laughed. "You're not going to start shushing me for their sake!"

She glanced back at the twins from the corner of her eye. That was the only way she ever looked at them. They had drawn pictures of her with triangles at the sides of her face, instead of eyes.

They had done so that very morning, just before Daddy came to pick them up. Of course it wasn't a surprise when he came, but their mother pretended that it was, anyway. Everyone knew she was just pretending. She never would have been up so early with a pink bow already in her hair unless she had known Daddy was coming. She would have been in bed with her eyes shut tight and the covers pulled up under her chin. The twins would have been downstairs in the kitchen, making milk puddles on the table and shooting soggy cereal back and forth with their spoons. Instead when Daddy rang the doorbell, it was clear everyone had been up for hours.

"Oh well," their mother had said when she

opened the door and saw Daddy standing on the porch. "Here you are. What a nice surprise."

From where the twins sat on the floor, it looked as though the entire horizon of fences and houses and back yards was balanced on Daddy's shoulders, as if he had come a long way to see them, carrying morning on his back. The bare branches of a maple tree poked up behind his head like antlers.

The twins laughed at that.

"I thought I would take the girls for a drive," Daddy said.

"A drive! How nice! What a nice idea. A drive." And their mother stepped back from the door so Daddy could finally come inside, although ever since he had stopped living there, he didn't like to go much beyond the threshold.

"Elspeth! Sabina!" their mother called, coming closer to them than usual and smiling wide. "Your daddy's here. He's going to take you for a *drive!*"

Elspeth and Sabina in their little dresses and white tights were too busy drawing pictures of Pearl to notice their mother at all.

"Girls! Isn't it exciting! To get to go for a drive with your daddy!"

Elspeth, without putting down her crayons, said, "Only if *she's* not going!"

Then Elspeth peeked out from behind her fine

blond hair, in time to see a smirk appear on her mother's face. At the same time Daddy's big fake-happy grin disappeared altogether.

"Why, honey!" their mother said. "What do you mean? Only if who's not going?"

"Her!" chirped Sabina, pointing at the drawing of Pearl, with her too tall hair and eyes like half-diamonds.

"Of course that awful woman isn't going. Your daddy wouldn't do that to his two favorite girls!"

Then their mother went off down the hall to get Elspeth and Sabina's matching jackets.

"Now have a great time!" she said, zipping them up and pushing them toward the door.

Daddy grabbed both of them in a big hug the minute they were outside, to show he was so happy to see them. "How are you, favorite girls?" he said.

Elspeth and Sabina giggled in Daddy's grip, as together they crossed the front lawn. A few leaves that had already fallen tickled around their ankles. It was very cold outside and the morning was already heavy with clouds.

"Maybe it isn't the best day to go for a drive, but I feel sure if we keep our fingers crossed these clouds will all get blown back where they came from," Daddy said. "Right?"

"Right!" shouted Elspeth and Sabina.

Daddy held onto them until they got to the car, so there was no way the twins could run back to the house when they saw Pearl sitting in the front seat.

"Now," Daddy said, "we're all set to have a great time!"

But Elspeth and Sabina refused to speak. They sat side by side in the back seat, staring angrily at Pearl's curlicue hair.

When the car backed out of the driveway and pulled away, their mother wasn't standing at the dining room window to wave goodbye.

"I'm bored," Elspeth said.

She said it whenever they passed through another town:

"I'm bored. This place is boring."

And Sabina added, "Are we there yet?"

The inside of the car smelled of bologna sandwiches and pickles, packed by Pearl in little paper bags.

Daddy drove north, toward the mountains. Every time they bothered to look out the windows, Elspeth and Sabina saw fewer houses, more trees and craggy stone walls. Sometimes little fields flashed by, where horses the color of chestnuts hung their sad long faces toward the road.

The Drive

"Those horses would be happier," said Elspeth, "if they were free."

"Sure," said Pearl, without turning around. "Maybe you could go and let them all out, Elspeth."

"I could," said Elspeth. "If Daddy stopped the car, I could."

Pearl had reached into her purse and taken out a flamingo pink tube of lipstick. The twins watched from behind as she painted her lips. They could see just her lips and a little bit of her nose reflected in the mirror she held up in front of her face.

"Sure," said Pearl. "That's fine. You let all those horses out of their yards, and what do you suppose happens then? They all starve to death. Or they walk across the road and get squashed flat. Hah!" Pearl sneered. "That's what happens, dear, when you set things free."

"The wild mustangs were free," said Sabina.

But Pearl didn't bother to answer. She was too busy putting away her lipstick.

Elspeth leaned over the front seat and tried to tickle Daddy's ear with her fingernail.

"Stop that, honey," Daddy said. "It's dangerous to do that when I'm driving."

Elspeth leaned forward even further, and scooped Pearl's purse into the back seat.

"Hey!" shouted Pearl. "Stop that! Give me that! Make them give me that back!"

"Take it easy," Daddy said. "They're just playing. Maybe it'll keep them quiet for awhile."

As he said this he put his hand over Pearl's knobby knee.

Pearl gave Daddy an awful look that came from her mouth and the corners of her eyes. "I won't forget this, Dave," she said. "I won't. You mark my words."

Daddy squeezed Pearl's knee and began to whistle.

The twins had opened up Pearl's purse. Nothing in it seemed very interesting. There were shreds of yellow Kleenex, a comb, the bright lipstick, empty gum wrappers, keys. They only liked the mirror, and so Elspeth threw the purse back onto the front seat.

"Thank God," said Pearl, and tucked the purse carefully under her heels.

Elspeth and Sabina tugged at the mirror. Sabina looked up once and said, "Are we there yet?"

Daddy didn't bother to answer, so Pearl and the twins looked out the dusty windows at the roots of the mountains. They passed grey houses that slouched into muddy lawns, toothy farm machinery that grinned uselessly in fields of yellow and brown stubble.

"Look at those leaves!" said Daddy. "Just look at

those colors! Almost as pretty as my two favorite girls!" Daddy laughed and Pearl pulled her bumpy knee out from under his palm.

"Why aren't we stopping yet?" Sabina shouted. "If we're here then why aren't we stopping?"

"Sure, honey," Daddy said. "Sure. We'll stop. The next place we see, we'll stop."

The wet road ticked beneath the wheels of the car. They went up a hill and around a thick stand of blotchy red trees and then Daddy saw a sign that said "Gifts. Horseback Rides. $3.00."

"Oh no," said Pearl. "No, no, no, Dave. They'll smell like animals all day. You know I can't stand that."

But it was too late. Daddy had already pulled the car off the road, and they all bumped up and down as it crossed the grass, finally coming to a stop beside a weary-looking wire fence. Behind the fence, a fat black pony wearing a saddle and halter nibbled at the grass. Its breath puffed out at the twins as they ran to lace their fingers through the loops of the fence.

A little further down the road was the white gift shop. Silver chimes in the shape of maple leaves hung in the windows.

"Jesus Christ, Dave," said Pearl, huddling and slapping her arms together in her wide fur coat. "It's too cold for this. When I said a drive I meant a drive, for God's sake, not a walk in the wilderness. But I should have known, I should always know better when it comes to you, Dave."

Daddy had turned his back on Pearl, and stood with the twins, leaning against the wire fence. The pony had stopped nibbling and half lifted its head to stare back at them. Pearl took a few steps toward Daddy, but then she stopped. Her heels wobbled too much on the rutted ground.

"Nothing's too good for my favorite girls," Daddy said, loudly.

A small man in a green parka emerged from the gift shop. He walked crookedly, with his head bent slightly to the left.

"Hiya," he said. "Come to take a ride?"

"Sure," said Daddy. "My favorite girls would like to take a spin on your pony."

"You bet!" The man in the green parka opened the gate and whistled. The pony swung its head away.

"Your horse would be happier," Elspeth said, "if he were free."

But the man in the green parka grabbed the halter and tugged the pony over to the gate anyway. Daddy picked Elspeth up by the waist and plopped her onto the saddle. Her short legs, plumply encased in the white tights, barely reached the stirrups.

The Drive

"Now it's your turn!" Daddy laughed, and grabbed Sabina. But Sabina struggled, flinging her legs around, trying to wriggle out of Daddy's grasp.

"No!" she shouted. "I want to sit in the front! Why does she get to sit in the front!"

Sabina's flying legs made contact: with the pony's dusty flank and with Daddy's chest. The pony shied away, its eyes rolled up white. Daddy let Sabina fall to the ground and leaned back against the fence, rubbing his chest.

The man in the green parka held the black pony steady, with Elspeth still swaying on its back. But then he turned to Sabina, never letting go of the halter.

"You can ride in front the next time," he said.

Sabina smiled coyly and got up from the ground, revealing a brown and green stain on the seat of her tights. The man in the parka lifted her onto the saddle behind her twin.

"Hold on, now!" he advised, and began to lead the pony slowly around the field.

Daddy and Pearl watched the pony's fat receding form. Little bursts of laughter from the twins reached them every now and then.

"There," said Pearl. "Now you see. Do you believe me now? Mark my words," said Pearl. "Whenever they come with us there's some kind of disaster!"

She stood precariously on her heels, separated from Daddy by the folds of the wire fence. Daddy was bent slightly, massaging his chest. He hadn't caught his breath yet.

Slowly, the pony led by the man in the green parka made its way around the field. As they passed Daddy and Pearl, the twins could hear Pearl talking.

"Maybe you'll mark my words, Dave. Don't think I'll hesitate . . ."

Her voice rose on the cold damp air, then faded like a spiral of smoke as the pony moved away.

Pearl was walking away from Daddy. She was walking unsteadily toward the white gift shop. Daddy watched her go without calling her back. The wind parted the fur of her coat and exposed the dark roots of her hair.

The twins laughed happily at the man in the green parka, who had now helped them to switch places on the saddle, Sabina in front this time.

Daddy looked at the ground.

Then he followed Pearl. They walked one behind the other along the road to the white gift shop.

Pearl was unaware of Daddy following her. She didn't slow down. Daddy could hear the maple leaf chimes ringing as she opened the door of the white building and disappeared inside.

Daddy sat down on the steps of the gift shop and

hugged his arms around his chest. Then after awhile he lit a cigarette. The man in the green parka came up, leading a twin with each hand.

"There y'go," he said, and grinned at Daddy. He looked very strange, grinning so much with his head bent toward his left shoulder. Finally Daddy handed him some money, and the man with the parka gestured toward Daddy's chest.

"Are you okay?" he asked.

"Sure," Daddy said, tossing his cigarette on the ground. "Just a little bruised."

"Better go inside," said the man with the parka. "Too cold to sit out here."

So Daddy stood up, and followed him into the gift shop. Immediately, everyone saw Pearl hunched over a glass case, peering at the turquoise jewelry inside it. The twins ran off in the other direction toward a rack of imitation Indian spears with rubber heads. Daddy snuck up behind Pearl until he was close enough to put his hand on the nape of her neck.

"Whatcha looking at?" he whispered.

Pearl gave a little jump. Then without turning she hissed "Nothing!"

But just the same, Daddy bought her a turquoise and silver ring before they left. Elspeth and Sabina stared silently as Pearl posed the hand with the ring on her hip or next to her hair so that the blue stone was always in their way.

They returned to the car, where they ate their bologna sandwiches with pickles, looking at the brown field and the lethargic pony.

Then Daddy started the car and they drove on. It seemed as though he had given up talking to Pearl and Elspeth and Sabina, he was so quiet sitting behind the steering wheel. The road turned between the mountains.

Pearl laughed softly to herself because there was nowhere for Elspeth to piss.

"What's to be so delicate for, for God's sake," said Pearl. "Just pull the car over to the side of the road, Dave. She can go behind a bush."

But Daddy thought that there might be a rest area around the next hill, so he continued to drive.

"Only the best," he said softly, "for my favorite girls."

As he drove, he occasionally caressed the spot where Sabina's foot had landed with the heel of one hand.

"Daddy," Elspeth insisted.

"Yes, honey," Daddy said. "I know."

"So delicate," said Pearl. "Why bother when they already smell like animals?"

The Drive

The car dipped down a side road along the edge of a mountain. The trees were so tall and the road so narrow that the sky disappeared behind startling red and yellow leaves.

"Dave!" Pearl protested. "Where the hell are you going?"

"There's a place to stop down here," Daddy said. "I remember it perfectly. A little amusement park and a petting zoo."

"You mean you've been here *before?*"

"I'm sure of it," Daddy said.

Rust and cream-colored birds flashed between the black tree trunks.

"Dave," Pearl said, "I don't think there's anything down here. Nothing."

Daddy winced a little bit, behind the steering wheel.

"What's wrong?" Pearl asked.

"Nothing," Daddy said vaguely. "Backache."

Sabina, leaning near the window, tilted the mirror back so that it reflected the leaves like delicate, bobbing faces. She laughed softly at the reflection.

"If you'd listened to me in the first place . . ." Pearl began, but then she let the sentence go, because the road before them suddenly grew narrower. Daddy had taken another turn-off and now the nose of the car was pointed straight down the side of the mountain, so that Pearl had to brace her arms against the dashboard.

"I think it was this road," Daddy said. "I remember these beautiful trees."

"Dave," Pearl said, "are you crazy? There's nothing here. Turn this car around right now."

"Daddy," Elspeth said, "are we almost there?"

"Yes, honey. Almost."

Daddy took another turn. Looking out the windows, Pearl and the twins could see the thick dark soil of the mountains pushed up between the twisted toes of the trees. The crabbed branches of pines hung nearly to the ground. In places, chunks of granite protruded from the earth, dripping shiny streams of water.

"I'm telling you now," Pearl said. "Turn this car around."

But Daddy wouldn't turn around. He wouldn't answer Pearl. His face was pale, so that the grey stubble on his cheeks looked dark. He clutched a cigarette, unlit, between his teeth.

"Daddy!" Elspeth shouted. "Daddy! I have to piss now! I have to go real bad!"

Daddy stepped on the brake so hard that everyone was thrown forward. The car swung half off the road and then stopped with two tires on the pavement and two in the dirt. Then Daddy leaned his head against the steering wheel. He rubbed his chest with the palm of his hand.

Because Daddy didn't speak, Pearl turned to the twins. "Well, I hope you're satisfied now," she said. "Get out of the car and *piss.*"

Elspeth and Sabina looked at each other and giggled. Elspeth pushed open the back door, and they ran out into the trees. They left the mirror lying, face up, on the seat. Pearl heard a faint childish voice call: "Don't peek!"

"Christ," said Pearl. "As if I'd want to peek. As if I have any reason on earth to peek."

But Daddy didn't respond. He leaned against the steering wheel, breathing hard.

"Don't give me any crap now, Dave," Pearl said. "After all I've put up with today and all the other days just like today. You mark my words, Dave, changes are coming. Mark my words!"

Daddy wouldn't mark her words. He wouldn't even answer. He had stopped rubbing his chest, though. Instead he tried to light his cigarette. Pearl noticed the way his hands shook.

"Dave!" she said. "What's wrong? Do you have a pain?"

Daddy nodded, wordlessly.

"Where's the pain, Dave?"

"Everywhere," Daddy said. He was breathing hard.

"Fine," said Pearl. "Fine. Don't tell me. You never tell me what I really need to know. And now I suppose I have to crawl around out in the woods to find those damn brats of yours."

Pearl made a loud sighing noise and shoved the door open. "I'll find them," she said, "and while I'm gone you can just get over that pain. It's nothing you didn't bring on yourself."

Pearl's heels sank into the velvety soil. She slammed the car door hard and wobbled off between the trees. "Men," Pearl was muttering. "Brats. Mark my words." Then she raised her voice to call "Elspeth! Sabina! Hurry up now! It's time to go!"

Branches scraped against each other. Leaves rattled. Pearl tiptoed a little farther between the trees.

"Elspeth! Sabina!"

Pearl thought she heard a giggle. She turned around and around. Bright maple leaves nodded at her, jeeringly.

"Cut it out now! Just cut out this game!"

Pearl pushed some branches aside. Drops of water splattered in her face.

"Dammit!" she shouted. "Stop this game or we will *leave you here!*"

She heard the sound of laughter, and so she shoved through more branches, and found herself standing on the edge of a stream with a rocky bed. Her heels tilted on the edge. She stepped back quickly.

"Elspeth! Sabina!"

But no one was there.

Pearl saw a pink ribbon float by on the water. It twisted gracefully over the rocks, twirled like a butterfly.

"Jesus Christ!" said Pearl, and began to follow the edge of the stream. She held onto slippery branches to keep her balance. A wet spider web stuck across her face, in her curlicue hair. She pawed at her face with her flamingo pink nails.

Another ribbon floated by on the stream.

"Elspeth! Sabina!"

Pearl's heels stuck in the ground. Her toes slid over rocks and roots. Leaves slapped in her face.

Oh Jesus," said Pearl. "Oh Jesus. Dave will never forgive me."

Her mascara began to run.

Suddenly, Pearl heard a voice.

"Our daddy would be happier," the voice said, "if he were free!"

But when she looked around, all Pearl could see were branches black and slim as pencil lines.

"Fine!" she yelled. "Fine! Just sit out here in the woods and wait for your daddy to come looking for you! Just stay out here! As if I could be bothered!"

Pearl slapped away the branches. She slapped her way back to the road, and saw that the car was still tilted halfway off the pavement, facing down the mountain. From where she stood at the edge of the trees, Pearl could see that Daddy hadn't moved at all since she left.

"Jesus!" said Pearl. "Men!"

She wobbled toward the car, toward the window on Daddy's side. She wouldn't get into the car again.

"All right, Dave," Pearl said to the window. "I gave you this chance. I've given you other chances. Now you'll get what you really want. You're *free*."

Pearl walked off along the road in the direction she wanted Daddy to turn the car. It was a steep road, and so Pearl had to stoop a little bit to climb it. But Daddy didn't watch her go. He didn't bother to massage his chest. He had let the unlit cigarette fall onto the front seat.

The wind parted Pearl's curlicue hair. It parted the fur on her coat, revealing the soft white underdown.

Elspeth and Sabina knelt beneath a pine tree in their white tights. They had pushed aside the fallen needles so that they could draw pictures of Pearl on the ground with their fingers. They were looking at each other, and laughing. Their blond hair hung free around their soft white faces.

• • •

Crazy Water

(Fragments of a Vacation)

*I*t rains because it must; and because I must, I watch them, these two women. I do not yet understand where one begins and the other ends, for they are as alike as two swans leashed with a golden chain. Graceful pale heads bent together, they are always whispering secrets. Because the sky is so darkly oppressive, their blond hair seems more bright, more mocking. From my window I see them leave the hotel every morning, holding up a blue umbrella that glistens wetly in the rain. Their hair is the brilliant color of hay; when I look down from my window at their white necks and golden heads I smell the hay, I sink into crackling, stabbing hay. I think that they feel my eyes: every morning they draw closer together and lower the blue umbrella as they pass beneath my window, and then they turn the corner, so that there is nothing left to look at, except the grey puddles on the sidewalk and, beyond the rooftops, the wider, writhing grey of the ocean.

I think that they are sisters, but I am not sure.

•

Whenever I come here, it rains. All the rooms of this hotel must smell of it, must combine the usual impersonal scent of rooms that belong to no one (having been occupied by many) with the penetrating stench of ocean and rain. There is a damp feel to the wood, a strange grittiness of the sheets that promises barnacles but delivers only unhappy nights spent tossing and turning, hair spread across the pillows like seaweed. At night here it is hard to distinguish the sounds of ocean from the sounds of rain, and many nights I have stayed awake trying to tell. I roll from one side of the bed to the other, guessing: this is ocean, this is rain.

I am unable to sleep. Sometimes I close my eyes, and then, in the morning, it is as if I have slept, because the dawn is a surprise. It rises like the broad shoulders of the one I have come here to forget, and startles me out of bed.

•

This is a large hotel; there are many rooms, many corridors carpeted with silence. I know the desk clerk, because of the times that I have been here before. Perhaps I continue to come back because of this, because I know there is a smile waiting for me with the desk clerk. She nods when she sees me, says, Well here's a familiar face. Yet the hotel is big enough that I could remain for days, going in and out, without ever seeing the desk clerk at all. I could commit a million crimes here, and none would be detected. In such a hotel it is impossible to know everyone, and yet it is comforting that the desk clerk knows me, and can smile. The other guests are phantoms, clacking keys and slamming doors.

They turn their faces away, when they pass me in the hall.

•

I first saw the sisters when I checked into the hotel. I had come in from the parking lot dragging my suitcases, those little leather anchors of my past, splattered with rain and startled by the stabbing scent of brine after so many hours shut in the car. They sat in the lobby together, on a black and red couch, the feet of one resting in the lap of the other, both of them reading. They held books in front of their faces with their white hands, every fingernail polished pink as coral. They wore green shorts that exposed their muscular, hairless calves and thighs, as if they thought the rain would pass and that they would soon be out running on the beach.

A very optimistic attitude, I remarked to the desk clerk.

She smiled and handed me my key. Yes, she said. And later they'll be out at the beach, whether it's raining or not. They do the same every day.

When I walked past them they looked at me. First one sister, then the other, lowered her book and raised her eyes as I went by. I felt the vivid blue of those eyes until the elevator carried me upstairs, and maybe even after that.

•

Every morning the color of their umbrella is reflected in the puddles on the sidewalk, and their feet stir ripples like miniature oceans. I crank the window open and lean with my nose pressed against the screen, feeling the sharp cold moisture on my face. I think of calling out to them, they are so alive in the rain.

•

At dinner I talk too much. The hotel dining room makes me expose more than I intend, because I am always relieved to reach it, to hear the whispers of silverware and unfamiliar voices. I am seated at a

table with people I have never met before, and I begin
to talk.

I have been to this hotel two times before, I tell
these strangers, so that now I have been here three
times altogether. Every time I have come not because
of the attraction of the place (although it has some
attraction; at any rate a place seems to become at-
tractive just because it is familiar, if you know what I
mean). But no, anyway, every time I have come here,
I have come to leave something behind.

This is what I tell them. As I talk I remember the
other two times: the interior of my car as I drove,
what spilled out of the suitcases when I dumped them
on the bed, the curtains in my room, the hairbrush I
left sitting on the bedside table with a twirl of hair
still caught in the bristles.

I continue: this time I am here to forget someone,
you know, a man; not just any man but a particular
one, although he was as generic as all the rest at
first, perhaps even more generic, I think that's what
attracted me to him in the first place, but at any rate
I soon needed to get far away. The moment he ceased
to be generic, I fled.

I stop talking to pick up my wine glass. In this
hotel every glass is a thing of beauty. I have picked
mine up many times already, and have become pre-
occupied with the appearance of my arm, whether

the movement of my arm is graceful enough as I reach for the wine glass.

You see I always seem to have that problem, I say. The minute they assert their individuality I flee. With this one it was worse than usual, maybe because he seemed more generic at first, and so the deception was greater. I expected him to stay generic, or, since he was so very generic at the start, to be less individual than usual at the end. But as it happened, the opposite proved true. He was more individual than they usually are. I began to have dreams about him, but not the kind you like to have. He would come and stand in front of me. I'd try to cover myself, because I was always naked, although he was not. He would stand and look at me and then he'd put his hand right here.

I demonstrate for the strangers by placing my own hand around my throat. Just like that, I say, and then I'd wake up. Soon I was having the dream every night, and then when I couldn't stand it anymore, I came here.

The strangers are appalled by my voice and by my story, because I have forced them to hear it. I sit with a man and a woman; evidently they are married, for they have begun to look alike, with greying hair and faces that are not quite wrinkled, but are loosening with middle age. I am alternately entranced by the buttons on the man's deep blue jacket and the dull play of light on his wife's pearl necklace. They say nothing, they smile a little bit, but their eyes protest. Unfortunately, it is too late, because I no longer care.

I meet a lot of them through my work, I say. You see I am a journalist, and because of that, I think, I have gotten into the habit of staring at people, of watching them. I used to do it on purpose, to help my work, and now I do it all the time, without thinking. They'd notice my staring, sooner or later they'd speak to me, before I knew it, I was involved. But I always keep open my option to flee.

Do you still dream? the man asks me, nervously. A white napkin is clutched in his hand.

It sounds awful, the woman adds.

No, I say. When I came here the dreams stopped.

I lean back in my chair and regard them. They are so serious, so frowningly attentive, that I have to laugh. I laugh and look around the dining room. Several tables away I see the sisters, looking at each other and then at me, smiling.

I'm very sorry, I say, rising from the table, to have talked too much.

And I hurry back to my room which, because I

have left my window open, reeks of the lightless depths of the ocean.

•

Unfortunately, it seems I carry the past with me when I travel. This is my misfortune. When I turn to unpack my suitcase I find, instead of the clothes I thought I packed, little bits of my past. I reach into the suitcase, thinking it is mine, and find things that I toss onto the rumpled bed: a compact, a broken sea-shell, the black and white knights from a chess set, a jeweled watch, a plastic comb with strands of hair tangled around the teeth, photographs of the one I have come here to forget (already he looks unfamiliar), unrecognizable shades of lipstick, ticket stubs from plays I have never seen. These objects loom out of the shadows imposed on the room by the curtains, which I have drawn in honor of the unpacking. But none of them are mine; they are mementos of a past I can no longer remember, or one I have not yet experienced.

I stand and stare at the things on my bed, and then there is a soft rap at the door. I am grateful for the interruption, even though I know it is impossible anyone could be visiting me, since I know no one. Therefore the knock is a mystery. I swing open the door and there is the hotel maid, in her uniform, pushing a cart stacked with clean linens. She has come to make the bed. We are surprised to see each other; she gives me a thin smile.

I have never liked to be in rooms with maids. They make me nervous, for they see too much, and too intimately, perhaps against their will. When I speak to them, I speak awkwardly.

There has been some kind of confusion here, I say, although what could have prompted it in a hotel like this, where every object is a thing of beauty, escapes me. A suitcase has been placed in my room which is not mine, and contains things that do not belong to me. I came here to rest; I don't want to deal with this inconvenience.

The maid stares at me, wishing I'd remove the dappled objects from the bed so she can work. No, she says. That's impossible, I'm sure. It's your suit-case, Miss, and no one else's.

She shoves the objects onto the floor, and sets to work, tugging at the sheets, as if I do not exist.

•

It is rare that I see one of the sisters without the other. Yet here is one of the two, alone. She leans against the glass door in the lobby, looking out at the damp street, then looking at her watch, while I, in the hotel gift shop, am only a few yards away. Many mornings I have wanted to call out to this woman, or perhaps to the other, so I know I must speak to her now, while I have the chance. I leave the gift shop and lean, too, against the glass door.

Every time I come here, it's rained, I say. Some people choose their vacations in just that way.

The woman turns toward me, and I am startled by her face: high cheekbones, as light and hollow as a bird's; white skin.

Yes, she says, some people do.

Evidently you choose your vacation that way too, I say. I've seen you and your sister around the hotel. The beauty of it is that the rain doesn't bother you, you go out anyway. As for me, I'm involved in a dialogue of forgetfulness: past loves and all that.

I think she is sympathetic, although something I've said has startled her; she blushes. She may smile, may even be friendly. Then suddenly the second woman appears in the hotel lobby. All at once my companion draws back from me, and her sister steps between us. She wears an ivory cross on a gold chain around her neck.

Come on, Resa, she says; she pushes the door open and the two sisters go out. They draw very close together and, although neither one looks back, I feel that they may be talking about me.

Crazy Water

•

The maid is making the bed, snapping the scent of clean sheets into the musty room. I stand by the window, because I do not like to feel in the way, and then again because I am watching the sisters come out of the hotel, arms around each other's waists, their feet splashing in the puddles.

These two sisters, I say, pointing out the window. I wonder if you know who they are. I think they may be old acquaintances of mine.

The maid stops her work, puts down a pillowcase, comes over to the window. The sisters are drawing away. The maid peers out of the window, looking where I point.

Sisters! she exclaims. Whores.

•

I sit at the desk, holding photos up to the light. His face is not familiar. I look from one photo to another.

Already, I have forgotten.

•

Since I find myself here again, I try to take an interest in things of the town: the dowdy main street with its white-painted gift shops, all reeking of scented candles and wicker, the opaque-windowed bars, the glass-fronted laundromats where women fold their clean clothes. The inhabitants of the town have a certain look. It is as if their faces have been bent by the rain and the wind, just like the crabbed black trees across from the bay. I seldom see the people speak. When the two sisters walk hand in hand through the shops, plucking up plastic lobsters, or bumper stickers, or polished shells, the shop proprietors stare at them with hostility; they are as out of place here as gaudy tropical birds, with their blue-shadowed eyelids and scarlet earrings. I move through the gift shops slowly, without expressing interest, and the sales clerks come to trust me. They rush to show me their cases of jewelry, tiny birds and frogs made out of seashells, seahorses dried and preserved, while the sisters remain utterly ignored. I can feel that the town turns to me, seeking some sort of justification for drabness. I am well liked; sometimes people stare at me on the street.

The desk clerk confides in me. I do not know her name, yet we smile at each other, and seeing that she is bored, I lean against the front desk. She tells me that the townspeople are worried by the rain. The ocean becomes strange when it rains so long, she tells me. Already the tourists have been complaining about the beach, odd things washing up on the sand, an unusual texture to the water, a peculiar aggressiveness in the tangling of seaweed around their feet. The rain makes the tourists bored, she says, and sinister.

On the contrary, I say. This place wouldn't be the same without the rain, to me at least.

The desk clerk looks at me strangely, and seems pleased by my concern.

One day, when I have been out exploring the streets, keeping the shimmering blue umbrella just ahead of me until it suddenly vanishes around a corner, I meet the desk clerk coming out of the lobby, tugging a windbreaker over her head. She urges me to follow her.

No one's in the hotel anyway, she says, if you'll come with me you'll see. You didn't believe me before, but now you will.

I believe you implicitly, I say.

But she does not hear me, for she hurries on ahead, body bent against the spitting rain; I run to catch up. We follow the road out to the beach, and as we walk I suddenly realize that we are not alone; groups of people in twos or threes are already following the road. There is a large crowd already on the beach. The desk clerk grabs my sleeve and pulls me through the crowd, until we stand at the inner edge of a wide half-moon of people, all pushing, leaning, struggling to see. At the center of the half-moon there lies, partially in the water, a whale that has been stranded by the tide.

The creature is calm, with placid sightless eyes, grey skin glistening in the rain. I think it is so wet that it cannot be suffering. An occasional tremor passes through its flesh. Barnacles crust on its fins and tail.

Two men are trying to push the whale back into the water, but it will not be moved; it seems almost to cling to the beach. Every time the huge body is finally rolled into the shallows the crowd cheers and expects the whale to begin swimming, but instead it is only pushed back onto the sand by the motion of the waves.

The desk clerk leans close to my ear. You see, she says. The ocean spits them out like afterbirth, and they won't go back.

My disgust at the sight of whale distracts me; I look around at the crowd, and suddenly I see the two sisters standing together at the far end of the half-moon. They are talking together, angrily. Then a girl darts past them out of the crowd and kneels beside the whale. She runs her hand along the dying animal so that the flesh quivers, follows the curve of its body to the tail, which she lifts off the sand to her lap. Her long black hair falls into her face as she leans forward. She examines the enormous tail closely, then makes a quick movement with her hand and jumps to her feet, letting the tail fall with a splat. The crowd murmurs, pushes forward to see what she has done, what she holds in her hand. They press so close that she cannot find a passage through, though she looks back and forth.

Mathilda! the desk clerk calls. Her voice, coming from so near, startles me. The girl comes toward us, smiling, and, stopping in front of me, she opens her hand. On her palm lies a razor blade, and a triangle of black flesh.

The desk clerk embraces the girl. Go home, Mathilda, she says gently, then moves aside so that she can pass. The crowd has lost interest in the beached and groaning whale, and now turns to surge after the girl, who, moving very quickly, has already disappeared among the dunes. I struggle to hold my place, but I am spun around again and again by the pressure of so many hurrying bodies.

Don't worry, the desk clerk says. They'll call someone from the aquarium to come about the whale.

But I am standing on my toes, pushing aside unfamiliar heads and shoulders, trying to see where the sisters have gone. Again the blue umbrella is lost to my sight.

•

I press my body into the sand so closely, so completely, that there are even a few grains in my mouth. The sun is on my back; it is the first sunny day of my vacation. From where I am lying I can hear the ocean and the sound of voices, down just below the dunes. I have seen what I should not see. By resting my chin in a hollow at the very top of the dune, I can look down at the two women on the beach, their white bodies entwined so inseparably that it is impossible to tell one from the other. Their soft crooning sounds come up to me like the cries of the sea birds. I should not watch, but I do, to see the one whose name I do not know press her lips to Resa's pale stomach. When they separate, Resa rolls away angrily and sits up, shaking the sand out of her hair. She speaks with such vehemence that I can hear her.

I don't understand, she is shouting. You know he blames me. You put me in danger, Barbara!

I cannot hear Barbara's reply.

You sacrifice me, Resa cries. If he comes here you know you have sacrificed me!

Barbara tries to touch Resa's face, but Resa draws away again, sits with her back to Barbara, legs drawn up and encircled by her thin arms. Barbara strokes her hair, rubs her back, but Resa will not turn; her blue eyes are fastened to the blue of the ocean.

I think, perhaps, she will be friendly.

•

Although I have forgotten him, I do not sleep. When I close my eyes I see hands twisting a white sheet, coiling it like a braid. I do not know whether they are my hands, or his, and because I do not know, I must keep my eyes open, all night.

•

The carcass of the whale remains on the beach, rotting in the rain. Efforts were made to save the puffing creature; again and again it was rolled into the water. Once, toward evening, it had seemed as if it would finally swim, but in the morning it was back on the beach again, dead this time. The stench reaches even the hotel, pervades all the comings and goings in the lobby and in the hallways with a strange, languorous sense of invasion.

Once they come out they never go back, the desk clerk says, shaking her head. Now it'll stay until it makes us all sick.

It is a thing not often experienced, I say. For me it increases the charm of the place.

The desk clerk laughs. But how long before everyone leaves the hotel? she says.

It seems to me that she is right; people will leave the hotel. The sickly sweet odor of decaying blubber now mixes with the scent of ocean and enters my room when I open the window, and it must be just the same for every other guest. Not all of them will be as tolerant as I am, and even fewer will inhale with perverse pleasure. Sitting in my room, I think about the whale, imagine the eyes dull and flat, the white barnacles, the tail with the missing triangle of flesh; I wonder what drew it to the sand. Yet I will not go out to the beach and look at it. I stay in my room and picture in my mind the black triangle in the girl's white palm.

Even the tide will not take the whale away; the ocean won't forgive its prodigals. Finally one morning the sun comes out, and the stench becomes unbearable. At last I go with the desk clerk to see the fishermen tow the dead whale out to sea.

This time there is no crowd. The whale is hideous, bloated, covered with sand and flies, surrounded by a darting flock of gulls. Two of the fishermen have chained it by the tail to the back of the motorboat, and they push it into the water until it begins to float. Then they signal to the captain of the boat, who starts the engine and begins to pull the corpse out to sea.

We watch until the boat and the whale become very dim on the horizon. One of the fishermen approaches us, for he has recognized the desk clerk.

We told him to take it way out, he says. Don't have to worry about it scaring the tourists anymore.

The desk clerk looks at him and smiles scornfully. We'll see, she says. Personally, I don't believe it'll ever go back so easily. Doesn't Mathilda have it by the tail?

The fisherman laughs, spits on the ground.

It'll never be back, he says.

·

I admit that I have followed them, without knowing why. Something about the blue eyes, the blond heads, perfectly matched, as if by the imagination of an artist. And then there is something more. I have seen them walking down the hall with their pale fingers tangled together. I have seen them stop before their door and search their pockets for the room key; I have seen Barbara before the door kissing Resa, bending Resa's head back, digging her fingers into Resa's hair. I know why the maids look away. Yet still I continue to follow, knowing that I have seen what I should not have seen.

I think that Resa could be friendly. I think that she could look at me with her blue eyes, which contain all the texture and fire of the sky, and listen to my stories. I think that she would lean toward me, bringing her blue eyes very close to mine, and explain to me all the things that I do not understand in my own stories.

•

I lean against the window. I insist, I say, that it is not my suitcase, and I demand to know what it is doing in my room.

The maid snaps the sheet and folds it sharply around the edges of the bed. She is tired of this question, will not answer it again. Instead she says, There was a man at the front desk this morning, asking for that friend of yours. He left something for her.

There is a funny curl to her lip when she says *friend*.

Resa? I ask.

No, says the maid, preparing to push her cart away. The other one.

She halts for a moment, staring at the photographs laid out on my desk in a row.

•

Is it not truly amazing, the lengths to which one's fate may take one, or rather, the great lengths to which one may take one's fate? Three times I have been drawn to this hotel, this time being, of course, the third. Yet the first time I saw it, squatting here by the sea, I had no idea that I would come back even a second time. I had been driving for miles, you see I had to get away, but I couldn't drive a minute more, and here was the hotel. So I stopped, and came in, nothing impressed me much in those days, I went straight to sleep without even suspecting how important this hotel would be to me. Still I think I don't realize its full importance.

The second time that I came here, I was vacationing with a friend, oh, a woman I am friends with no longer, you see I do not find it easy to have friends; that is my misfortune. I like them for a while, some of them more than others, some very much indeed, but after a while the novelty of having a new friend wears off, and it all becomes so routine: these phone calls, little day trips, lunches and dinners spent discussing the same trivial problems again and again. I guess it is true that I tire of people rather quickly. Perhaps it is all my fault, but I don't think so. Rather I think it has been my fate to meet only tiresome people. Eventually they can tell I am disillusioned, and they drift back into their own lives. Nevertheless, I liked the friend with whom I took this vacation, at least at the time we set out. We had some things in common, each of us fleeing our respective lives. Once the vacation was over, I didn't enjoy her anymore. She spent the whole time complaining about the rain, which I, for some reason, liked. I couldn't stand to hear her complain! I would have done anything to shut her up, and was comforted only by the knowledge that she was temporary. I never saw her again after we came to this hotel, and never wanted to.

And now here I am again. You'd think, having had such a bad experience here the last time, that I would never come back; but on the contrary, I'd never think of going anywhere else. I have been here three times, and I have never enjoyed myself. Yet I feel compelled to return. I have come here this time to forget about a man. Until I came, I dreamed about him constantly. In my dream he always lay next to me, asleep, while I sat up in the dark and could not sleep at all. Always as I looked at him I was furious that he could sleep and I could not. I was touched by the way his eyes looked when they were shut in sleep, his eyelashes seemed so long and soft that I hated him. He was always lying on his back and I hated him so much for sleeping while I was awake that I would reach out and put my hands around his neck like this—

And I demonstrate on my own neck for Barbara and Resa, who do not want to listen, who keep their blue eyes on their dinner dishes, but who listen never-theless.

But then, before I could kill him, I would wake up. I had this dream so often that I was afraid I would wake up and find that I really had killed him. Finally I had to leave, and so I came here. Now I don't dream about him anymore.

The two women, both dressed in white, fidget like birds in a cage, wishing they could flee, dragging their eyes away from mine. They will not answer, will not speak, yet I feel that Resa is sympathetic. I saw them the moment I entered the dining room; their white dresses glowed like pearls in the dim light. Now, sitting with them, I feel ugly, awkward, almost masculine. Their beauty is terrifying.

I know this man is now looking for me, I continue, and yet he has no idea where I am. He has no idea why I left. I never told him about my dreams, why should I? What business is it of his, as long as I didn't kill him? Eventually he'll forget about me; it's easy to find someone new.

Suddenly Barbara stands up, tossing her napkin on the table, and walks angrily away. I am left alone with Resa, who finally must meet my eyes.

I'm sorry, Resa says. It's just that she is so afraid of being replaced.

Can I replace her? I ask.

No, Resa says. She will never be replaced.

•

For the first time, when they pass beneath my window, their hair glints in the sun. They wear shorts and blouses, have sweaters tied around their waists. They have their arms around each other. I am startled by the knotted muscles in Resa's arms, which I had always thought as fragile and breakable as smooth china.

•

Angry words pass between them, the name of a man. I am sheltered in the dunes. I can look down at their white bodies, so tense with hate. I see the horizon, the harmonious meeting of sea and sky, all blue splattered with clouds and gulls and breakers, finally invaded by the two women. They run from the beach and dive into the water, disappearing momentarily under the soft waves, then emerging again in deeper water, only a few yards apart. They shout and laugh to each other, and so I know that they are reconciled. I am disappointed by their reconciliation, and so I sulk in the dunes, rolling over in the sand onto my back, turning my gaze straight up, as though they might feel my snub. I am sleepy, swollen by the sun; I could sleep here, in the dunes, and never return to the hotel. Finally their voices draw me back. Now they are even farther from the shore; there is a wide space between them, but they wave to each other. Resa begins to swim toward Barbara, her body cutting the water with the grace and speed of a shark. Soon the two heads bob close together, and I wonder if they are embracing under the water.

I begin to doze, and then when I open my eyes again, I am not sure what I have seen. The two women are playing games in the water, swimming around each other, pouncing on each other's shoulders with shouts of joy. Resa swims behind Barbara and puts her hands on Barbara's head, then pushes her under the water. There is no cry, little struggle, so it seems they are still playing. Once Barbara seems to escape, and her face appears, her mouth open, gasping for air. Then Resa has grabbed her again, pushes her down. Finally Resa, too, dives under the water. She emerges alone, and swims with calm strokes to the beach. There, she begins to dry herself with a pale blue towel.

•

In the morning, I walk down on the beach, to see what I can find in the sand.

•

My darling:

You do everything so well, so completely, but perhaps, in this instance, not completely enough: as you can see I have your address, obtained so easily from that woman in your office—you know, the one with the paperweight containing the two seahorses, the one who always wears the grey skirt. You are so fond of confiding in her, but then, once she told me (she did not wish to tell me), it seemed that I should have known. Where else would you go?

Of course none of this is important now; all that truly matters is you, my darling, and this absence, which has gone on for much too long. I am acutely stung by your empty chair, by the scraps of paper you left behind, by your ring (it waits for you safely, here on the windowsill, above the sink). I wish that you would come back; I wonder what it is that you saw or thought you saw that sent you away so quickly. I hope that you are reconsidering, there in your room, where you have evidently found company that you prefer to mine. You should ask yourself, darling, how many times you have seen, only to realize that you imagined all along.

My love, do not forget that I know where you are. You know well enough, I will not wait forever.

• • •

Tenure Track

*I*t was only noon, and already Stephen and Laura had been lost six times. They laughed about it, decided they were good at it, then realized, bookishly, that it was a sort of metaphor for their lives. Outside their windows, Connecticut rolled by in fecund puffs of green that blocked out incidentals, like road and sky; their bright small landscape included only the fertile leaves, a scattering of maps, the steering wheel, and their tanned affectionate knees, jousting playfully for space beneath the dashboard.

Laura had spread the best map across her thighs; she held it delicately, as if it were an illuminated text summoned with great reluctance from the depths of a mysterious archive. She had a theory about getting lost. "They roll up the roads," she said. "Every night, after we go to sleep, they roll up the roads, and then in the morning, before we wake up, they roll out new ones." She glared suspiciously out the windows, pretending to look for furtive New Englanders with rolls of asphalt on their backs, sneaking off into the farmlands.

It was silly but there was something true in it, and they both laughed, because in the sunshine it was easy to laugh about being lost. They had been lost dozens of times since they moved east. Simple things, like finding the grocery store, confounded them. They'd been lost in other ways too, ways they preferred not to acknowledge. And finally they were in a place where it made sense to be lost.

"I hope she won't be upset with us," Laura said. She folded up the map and rubbed her sweaty palms against her jeans; she was nervous. Meeting people always made her nervous, and when Stephen could tell she was nervous, he tried to make her feel better.

"I'm sure she'll understand," he said. He was nervous, too, but he liked to pretend that nothing concerned him unless it was written down and pressed between book covers, and sometimes he pulled it off.

And it seemed that he succeeded. Laura pulled her fingers through her short tawny hair, yawned, and made a hat out of the map.

"Do you think there'll be many people there?" she asked, childishly—just like a child wondering about Christmas presents.

"Oh, yes," Stephen said. "It was always a great affair, the Misses Morkan's annual dance."

Laura scowled at him. She hated it when he got professorial with her.

"Stop that. Who'll be there?"

"Oh honestly," Stephen said. "Do you think I'm her social secretary or something? They'll be there. All of them. Everybody."

Laura turned her face to the window and watched the sheep go by. "That's too bad," she said. "Whoever *they* are, I hate them. I hate them all." She imagined the sheep all in neckties, or dresses with big flouncy scarves, discussing James Joyce over trays of hors d'oeuvres. There was always some poor undergraduate in a French maid costume carrying the tray. Laura hated the French maid worst of all.

She turned abruptly back to face him. "What do sheep eat with cocktails, anyway?" she asked.

Stephen sighed. "At least try to be good," he said. He realized that he sounded pedantic. It was like telling students about punctuation; he was bad at it. He didn't punctuate, himself. "She's a Very Important Woman, Laura. She could be a Very Valuable Friend."

Laura sat back quietly in her seat, like a child chastised. She placed the map hat over her face, and intoned deeply into the cone (Worcester, Massachusetts, lay just right of the pinnacle): "You're full of shit, Dr. Lewis."

She lowered the map. "I think that was your literary conscience speaking, honey."

Stephen didn't reply. He concentrated very hard on very important things: the steering wheel, the speedometer, and the road, dappled dark with shadow trees.

In fact he was annoyed because he didn't know who would be there. It was the first time since coming east that he and Laura had been invited to something purely social. They'd drifted through campus cocktail parties, but those were formalities, the stuff of business. For a month he had felt it sharply: his colleagues hid from him behind their elegant stemware, raising toasts and passing martinis, offering food without friendship. He had begun to wonder if he had made a mistake, coming so far, dragging Laura with him to this craggy coast; but it was a very good job he had taken, and he wanted very badly for it to work. Then at last: friendship proffered, and the invitation accepted.

"For God's sake, Laura," he said, "it's not like she's just *anybody*. It's the President's Wife, for God's sake."

A row of willow trees bowed down outside the car windows.

"I know it," Laura said, sulking; she wanted to sulk. She sulked because she was jealous of the President's Wife, of all women like the President's Wife: women who married important men and then wore the importance everywhere, traded on it. Laura imagined their lives in the same way that she sometimes imagined the interiors of houses as she passed on the sidewalk, peeking in windows: behind those demure draperies lurked worlds of privilege, of luxury, a life without problems, without slamming doors and curdled milk—stockings without runs, the perfect egg yolk every morning. "It's just that I want to *be* her, and if I can't *be* her, then I want to *kill* her."

"That's very antisocial of you, honey," Stephen said.

The road dipped down into a deep glade of trees. Gnarled stems and rubbery green protuberances snuggled intimately toward the pavement. Driving like this, lost, it was easy to imagine that the passage would close up behind them and disappear—once through it, they'd never go back. New England revealed as a kind of fairy land where passing academics were folded away into cicada-throbbing jungles; or perhaps where those ambitious enough to undertake the search might find a cave of treasures, a fairy godmother dripping with grants and sabbatical leaves . . .

"The thing is, you never know how someone like this can help you," Stephen said. As he said it he knew that he sounded opportunistic, like an old campus careerist clawing for "the right connection." He sounded like the people he and Laura had mocked back in Chicago. So many nights they'd returned to their apartment, bent double with wine and joyous mockery. And now here he was, plunged deep in this obscure woodland, chasing after a college president's wife like a hound after a scented rag.

He couldn't help it; he knew he was lost; so he kept on.

"Of course you still have to do your homework, like everybody else," he said. "But who you know *can* help. Just look at Bocklin back in Chicago. Just look at Gerard up at Buffalo. Talented, sure, but who isn't? Connections are everything, Laura. It never hurts to have friends . . ."

"In important places," Laura said, finishing his sentence. She had slumped down underneath her map headdress; maybe, Stephen thought, she was studying new routes under there, figuring out what turns they ought to take. Maybe she'd emerge from under that brightly colored cone of paper and point the way for him.

A tiny grocery with a screen door and a hand

painted sign (Videos & Bait) flashed up beside them.

"I think we ought to stop," she said, "and ask directions, Dr. Livingstone."

Stephen supposed she was right.

The screen door was torn and the place was dark, dank, smelling of mothballs and mold. In the gloom Laura and Stephen could make out shelves crammed with Gold Medal flour, hamburger extender, and red plastic fire trucks, all of it covered with a frosty patina of dust. Likewise the young man who lounged unpromisingly behind the dirty counter.

Stephen rattled the map and Laura's hat turned horizontal. "Excuse me," he said, speaking slowly and clearly, but without much hope, as he might address a class of freshmen, "can you tell us how to get to Route 115?"

The young man reached for the map and began to speak eloquently upon the topic of routes: dirt, gravel, and paved. Laura drifted away between the shelves. At the back of the grocery she suddenly found herself nose to lip with a big writhing bucket of earthworms. Above it was a sign: Live Bait.

Laura gazed tenderly at the roiling brown sea. It reminded her of childhood, of rainy days when the worms rose to the surface of her mother's sodden flower garden. Life had seemed so promising.

In a minute Stephen came up behind her with the jaunty air of a traveler. He saw her staring. "Need some live bait?" he asked.

"No, darling," she said. "I'm sure I'll be baited aplenty when we get to this social extravaganza. If we get to it."

She turned archly toward the car. Stephen trailed silently behind her, out of the grocery, across the dirt lot. Silently, he started the car.

The silence made Laura think that perhaps she had gone too far. Without the map to hide behind, she had to depend on words. As they pulled away, she gestured toward the store. "Speka da ingles?" she asked, pulling a dopey face.

"In fact," Stephen said, "the young man was surprisingly well informed."

"Ah."

"The problem, it seems, is that the roads we've been following, as marked on *this* map," he indicated her former hat, "do not, in fact, exist. To be exact, this map has shown us *dirt* roads. Thus our mutual confusion. Thus our mutual lateness."

Laura felt blamed, as if she'd drawn the map as well as worn it, but she knew that she'd been naughty, so now she was quiet. The worms had made her feel superior. For a moment, back there in the store, she'd felt above it all—above him, especially.

But the superiority, along with the worms, drew farther and farther behind her as the car progressed
up the road. Soon pride and "live bait" alike were
swallowed up by yet another tangle of green; the
car turned an ambiguous corner, plunged downhill,
passed a sign for the town limit.

"Now," Stephen said with satisfaction, "we're on
the right track!"

Laura's stomach drew tight with dread, but she
knew that Stephen felt badly about it all, and when
she knew that, she tried to make him feel better; so
she said nothing. The part of her that had reveled in
being lost, that longed to remain lost with him in this
narrow world of forest and dashboard for the rest of
the day, the rest of the night, perhaps always, was si-
lenced.

"What's she like?" she asked.

Stephen was pleased. "She's very nice. She's very
down to earth. She's very . . . normal."

"Just like us," Laura said.

Stephen looked toward her to see if she were jok-
ing, but her expression was serious. She was contemplating leaves and bushes with great seriousness.

Suddenly he stopped the car. "This is it!" He
backed it up so fast that a cloud of dust billowed up
from the tires.

"You're a sharp-eyed one!" Laura said. Although

she'd been staring avidly at the greenery, she hadn't even seen the little mailbox jutting out between the trees bearing the honored name and number. Just beyond the mailbox was a dirt driveway that wound up through the forest and into obscurity.

Stephen hesitated. "D'ya think this could be it?" he asked, wrinkling his forehead and turning a little piece of white lined paper, the stuff of student notebooks, around in his hands. On the paper was a barely decipherable scribble: the very incorrect directions given by the President's Wife.

"You'd think she'd know where she lives," Laura said, reproachfully.

Stephen ignored her. "Well, this is the number; and this is the street. I guess this is it."

"I reckon so, Mr. Clark."

He turned the car up the hill.

The driveway was steep and full of ruts. Together they jounced and rattled up between the slender trees, packed here so tightly, Laura thought, that a rabbit couldn't pass between the trunks. At each corner they expected to see the house; but the house eluded them, and the road continued to climb. Everything was in shadow; the sky seemed to have withdrawn. It became a tiny slash of blue, very far above them.

At last, just when they had agreed to turn back, there was the house.

It crouched against an outjutting of rock, as if it had grown there; it was grey, and weathered, and had a great preponderance of windows. It was like anybody's summer house, Laura thought: there was the rusty barbecue, resting by a clump of shrubs, there was a tennis racquet, cast down into the grass (she thought maybe the grass had grown up through the tennis racquet, but that must be wrong; clearly the tennis racquet had just been thrown there after a humiliating defeat on the courts), there was the row of fishing rods leaning against the wall. And yet something seemed to be wrong.

Suddenly, Laura realized what it was: shutters were hanging. Over in a corner was a dusty stack of bricks, as if somebody had intended to pave the walk but had forgotten. There was a bird feeder on a green pole, but no birdseed in it. The place was dumpy.

"What a strange place to live," she said.

But Stephen hadn't noticed the house yet. He was glancing around nervously.

"Should I park here?" he wondered. "No one else has. Do you think it's all right to leave the car here?"

"Where else?" Laura said, raising her eyebrows,

and waiting for him to notice the unimaginable: the President's House was a Dump.

He continued not to notice. "Yes, yes, of course. Where else would I park? The road's really too narrow, no one else will be able to get by if I park there . . ."

"Poor Stephen," Laura said, rubbing his shoulder. "So young, so eager to do the right thing . . ."

He cut the engine, and they stepped out of the car.

They had expected to be greeted by shouts, or the meaty "pock" of tennis balls, or the clinking of ice in five dozen glasses of whiskey, or the rumble of intellectual conversation pitted by a few off-color howlers; instead they were greeted by silence, then the buzzing of insects numerous but invisible, then an enigmatic plash revealing the nearness of water. They walked forward, toward the house, and suddenly could see the pond behind it, more green than blue, thanks to an immense enthusiasm of water lilies. A sagging dock reached tentatively out into the froggy muck.

Suddenly, Stephen, too, realized that something was wrong.

But before he could say it, a door opened, and through it emerged the President's Wife. She swept down upon them in her gauzy lounging dress like an entire swarm of butterflies, sleeves fluttering every-where.

"Steve! You're here! I'm delighted! This must be your wife, Lauren!" She offered Laura her hand, but withdrew it without touching. "The directions were fine, I'm sure? Since you're here, after all . . ." Her voice faded into a giggle.

"It's Laura," Laura said.

"Pardon?" The President's Wife peered closely through her glasses; the lenses magnified her eyes.

"Laura, not Lauren."

"Oh! That's all! I'm sorry, dear, sorry. It's still delightful to see you, though, isn't it? Come on into the house!"

There was no time for a reply; she disappeared inside ahead of them. Laura had just enough time to pull a face at Stephen before they stepped through the door into the President's House.

All at once they were inundated: by a smell like rotting apples, by strange ominous piles of *stuff*, packed everywhere (in the narrow entryway, along the walls, on tables and chairs and counters), and by the voice of the President's Wife. The voice carried them through the first dangerously leaning piles of junk like a raft crossing the River Styx; and on the other shore there was more and more and more junk—room after room of junk, it seemed to Laura and Stephen, as they trailed along after the voice. The President's Wife receded before them, room by room, just as her house had receded before them at every bend in the road. They'd catch sight of her gauzy sleeve, and she'd be gone, around another corner. But the voice—the voice—that voice!

"I told Harry you were coming—you know, I'm so excited to have you come! I want *desperately* to show you my newest acquisitions, Steve. I'm dying for your opinion. It's so nice to have someone new on the faculty, a new face, new ideas, new opinions, new friends. Believe it or not, Steve, I don't entertain all that much. This is a real treat for me. You know that I just got back from abroad, don't you? Oh, of course, what on earth am I saying! I just told you about my new acquisitions, sure you know I've been traveling . . . I always get so breathless when I travel, don't you? So much coming and going, to-ing and fro-ing . . ."

In the dim light, Laura reached out to poke one of the piles of stuff, and her fingers sank into a strange, soft warmth.

"Stephen!" she hissed and grabbed his hand, to dissuade him from the siren.

"Laura! Don't be ridiculous!" Stephen said, shushing her, although it was impossible that anyone could have heard, over that voice; impossible that there was anyone to hear, among so many piles, with so little light, and that smell of rotting apples.

"It's so stuffy in here! I'm so sorry, Steve, that it's so stuffy. But I've been abroad, you know, and so the house hasn't been open. Harry stays in town most of the time, to be close to all you folks. He's a real homebody. But I'm one for travel. That's one of the real contradictions of our marriage, you know."

The voice suddenly took root, and all at once Laura and Stephen found themselves in the kitchen, looking at the wide gauzy rump of the President's Wife as she bent over to peer into the refrigerator.

She popped out of it smiling, with a piece of smoked fish on a little china plate. "I'm talking awfully fast, aren't I?" she asked. "I'm being awfully rude. I don't mean to be. Would you like a snack? I've got plenty of food. And a drink? We must get you a drink after your long drive. Wine? Beer? Vodka? Let's go out on the patio."

Laura and Stephen looked out of the President's kitchen window at the President's patio; and beyond it, to the President's dock, where the President's canoe quivered among the President's water lilies; and beyond that, across the President's verdant lagoon; and beyond that, to . . . nothing. There was no faculty, no Dean of Students, no huffy Provost, no undergraduate dressed like a French maid, no tennis players, no lousy academic jokes.

"Oh, I'm so sorry!" Laura squeaked—she knew she was squeaking, she knew she shouldn't squeak, but she couldn't help it. "We're *early!*"

The President's Wife didn't hear; she had dipped back into the refrigerator, proffering once again her prodigious silken backside; and once again she emerged, this time bearing a little round container of *onion dip.*

"You can call me Margot, dear," she said. "That'll be perfectly fine."

Dip and fish were arranged on a plate with crackers; and Laura and Stephen likewise were arranged upon the President's patio, in white chairs darkened by grit and festooned with the weavings of spiders yet unseen. Margot (self-christened with such familiarity, Stephen thought) disappeared in and out, frenetically, waving her butterfly sleeves.

"My goodness," she said, planting her hand on her forehead in mock consternation. "There's something I'm forgetting. Definitely, I'm forgetting something. What is it, Steve? Oh! of course!"

She disappeared again, then reappeared laden with bottles: a magnum of white wine, a pint of vodka, something pink that Laura imagined would taste like flowers. She was about to say so, when she caught a look from Stephen.

"Be quiet," the look said, "it's *the President's Wife!*"

But his mouth said, "This is a lovely place, Margot. You and Harry are so lucky to have your own pond."

Laura could see him savoring the names: *Margot* and *Harry*, rolled on his tongue and sucked toward his tonsils, just like the wine. For a moment she felt superior again, contemplating him as she had contemplated earthworms roiling in a tub.

"It would be much nicer, Steve, if Harry would take care of the water lilies. Do you know that water lilies double every day? It's true," she sighed, with mock sorrow. "Twice as many tomorrow as today. Harry hasn't treated them in *three years,* you know."

Laura giggled, and felt with satisfaction the touch of the sun on her shoulders, despite the smell of the pond, there beneath her feet. In the sun it was easy to forget everything rotten, to ignore the inexorable progress of water lilies. Stephen sipped his wine with a look of confusion.

Margot evidently took it for disdain. "It's not one of the finer labels," she said. She turned the bottle so that Laura and Stephen could see the price tag.

"Oh, don't worry about him," Laura said. "He'll swallow anything. Won't you, Odysseus?" She prodded him in the side, laughing and turning her face up toward the sun.

There was a silence. Then Margot poured herself a vodka. "I've been talking so fast," she said. "This'll slow me down." She swallowed it; poured another.

Encouraged by the cheap brew, Stephen decided to put forth his question: "Where is everyone?"

Margot squinted behind her glasses. "I told Harry you were coming," she said. "He promised to join us. I told him, 'Harry, this delightful young man works for you—there he is, sitting up there in that squeaky ivory tower of yours, and you don't even know him. Shame! Shame! Shame!' " Margot shook her pale fat finger. "So he said he'd come. I intimidated him, I'd say!" She leaned back in her white chair, blond and resplendent as a monarch, and Stephen blushed to imagine it: he was new in town, and already a topic of conversation at the President's breakfast table.

"I'm sure Harry appreciated it," Laura said, reaching forward to tear off a bit of smoked fish with her fingers.

"Savage!" Stephen said.

Laura smiled sweetly and chewed the fish.

At that Margot began to talk again: of her travels, of her "acquisitions," of the friends she'd made abroad, of the money she'd spent and intended yet to spend, of the interesting sights she'd seen and how breathless they made her . . . Yet it was impossible to tell what it was she had acquired, or just where it was she had been. It all flowed around them in a miasma of talk, which, Laura decided, wasn't really so unpleasant if you broke it down to sound, to syllables, to raw consonants and vowels and rhythms, if you thought of it as music, filled with harmony or discord depending upon the whim of the composer, but meaning . . . nothing. Margot poured as she talked; she refilled Stephen's wine glass again and again; Laura's, which remained full, she passed over in favor of her own, which was constantly emptying and refilling, first with vodka, then with wine, then with the pinkish liqueur, which smelled (as Laura had suspected) of flowers.

Abruptly, in the midst of all her talking, Margot fell silent; she eyed the pond.

"It would be so much nicer if Harry would do the weeds," she said. Then, just as suddenly, she stood, with the glass of something pink balanced on her palm. "So what!" she cried. "So what! We can still do it! Steve, Lauren—we must go out in the canoe! It's a wonderful experience, the canoe! Of course I don't want to force you. But, well—yes, I do! I do want to force you! We must go out in the canoe! I'll get us hats!"

She ran into the house, banging the door behind her.

"Stephen," Laura said. "I don't want to go. I'm not going."

Stephen only shrugged, and regarded the toe of his left shoe. He had put on his new shoes for the visit, and now there was a brown cake of mud on the toe. "Well," he finally said, "she *is* the President's Wife."

The door banged, and she was among them once again, her arms festooned with hats. Stephen selected a softly slouching fisherman's hat; Margot put on a wide-brimmed straw hat dyed with alternating rings of purple and orange. Silently Laura regarded the final hat, resting in the crook of Margot's elbow.

"No thank you," she said, primly.

"Come, come, dear," Margot piped. "You'll get sunstroke. This isn't a fashion show, is it? Who cares how you look—you're among friends!"

"No thank you," Laura said. For a moment it was not altogether clear what she had turned down. Then she turned back to tug at the smoked fish.

Margot seemed not to have heard—indeed, she

seemed to have forgotten Laura altogether.

"Come on, Steve. You can sit in the front, with those strong arms of yours, and I'll steer." They headed down the steep bank toward the dock, leaving Laura on the patio. Stephen looked back at her—it seemed to Laura that the look invited her to change her mind. Instead she frowned, and silently mouthed two words: "She's crocked!" Stephen pretended not to understand, and climbed into the fore end of the President's canoe.

Laura continued chewing as they pushed off awkwardly from the dock, as the silver canoe threaded through the green and white fabric of lily pads. She finished the smoked fish as they rounded a curve in the pond (her fingers were oily now; they smelled of fish, of rot, of death). As the canoe receded behind a bend she started on the onion dip. The crackers were damp, but she smeared them with dip, one after another, just the same. At last the canoe vanished; only the euphoric trill of Margot's laugh remained, magnified across the water like the mating cry of a bright exotic bird in the green jungle.

Alone at the edge of that big humid house, Laura felt suddenly afraid. When the canoe had first pushed off—when it had first become clear to her that Stephen really intended to go without her—she had imagined herself running through the house, opening it up: every drawer, every closet, every cabinet, every book, every envelope. She'd read every letter, she'd examine every glass, she'd even lift the cover off the butter dish; she'd prod her way to the top and bottom of every mysterious stack of stuff, until she finally found the essence of it—the essence of being the President's Wife, the wife of a powerful man. But now that she was finally alone, she couldn't do it. She was afraid; Stephen had left without her.

As if summoned by her unhappy thoughts, a spider sidled out onto the patio; it crept out from between two boards, extending its black legs first, like fingers. The legs were as long as fingers, Laura thought; the body was thick, meaty, ovoid, and black as an olive. She screamed and jumped up, knocking over her chair. She retreated, in spite of herself, into the house.

Inside it was silent, smelly; a clock vibrated on the counter. The house was thick with the sense of invasion, as if it could feel Laura there—as if it might try to push her out. Laura leaned on the counter, then on the sink. She opened the refrigerator. It was empty, except for a few bottles of beer and diet soda and a wedge of cheese, still wrapped in plastic. In the freezer she found a red hail of tiny tomatoes; nothing else.

In a cabinet were more bottles: vodka, rum, whiskey, brandy, brandy, brandy. There were boxes of crackers, all opened, none empty. In the drawer, the usual silverware, all of it gritty; a rusty spatula; a knife caked with dried egg.

The inside of an upper cabinet was plastered with bits of paper: little notes, newspaper advertisements, a cut-out photo of a popular television journalist. They were ragged bits, as if torn and taped carelessly there. Laura saw that tuna was on sale, two cans for a dollar, that the horse jumping finals were being held in Newport, that mold spores were worst in August. Sentences, written in Margot's hand, were taped there, too: "take 3 before bedtime," "groomer's hours, 8:30 to 1:30," and, in the midst of it all, her own phone number, her husband's name.

Laura stared at her number. It seemed strange, almost mystical, taped up like that inside the cabinet of a stranger. The cut-out television journalist stared back at her through elegant Asian eyes—cold eyes that made no claims for Margot's sanity.

She slammed shut the cabinet, and ran outside.

She ran down to the pond's edge in time to see Stephen and Margot paddle up to the rickety dock. For a moment she thought that they would walk across the lily pads and back to the shore—the green deceiving mass seemed that solid. Instead they carried out the minor gymnastic necessitated by the

shaky connection of boat and dock, stepping awkwardly, tentatively, like ducks, she thought, onto the
wood. Stephen was smiling, sweating—soaking wet.
Margot likewise, her plumage sopped with stinking
pond water.

"Gone fishin'?" Laura asked.

"No harm, no harm, no harm done!" Margot sang
out, and ran toward the house, arms flapping. "We
have to change for dinner anyway!"

Stephen stooped to tie the canoe. Laura, behind
him, prodded his damp buttocks with her toe.

"I want to go," she said—whispered, so that the
President's Wife wouldn't hear.

Stephen rose slowly, professorially, having ignored the digit in his posterior, with an attitude that
suggested he was prepared to ignore much more.
"Margot wants to show us her new acquisitions," he
said.

"She's a loon," Laura said.

"It would be rude," Stephen said.

"She's drunk," Laura said.

"For that matter," said Stephen, ever the pedant,
"so am I."

And so they trudged, one after the other, up the
slippery slope to the President's patio. Midcourse in
the mud, Stephen leaned a confiding lip to Laura's
ear: "This," he whispered, "is the *President's hat!*"

She, cold with disgust, did not respond, but imagined other digits, vengefully employed.

Gaining the top step, they saw that Margot had exchanged her damp Madame Butterfly for a sumptuous rust-colored robe, tied around the waist with a yellow woven belt weighted by a cluster of thick silky fringe, like a lamp tassel.

"Margot," said Stephen, reverently, "that's *lovely*."

She twirled around on the top step. "It is, isn't it? It's one of my newest. What do you think, Lauren?"

"It reminds me of something," Laura said, diplomatically.

Margot blinked behind her glasses. "I'm sure we'll find something to suit you, dear," she said. "I have so much stuff. Why, acres and acres and acres . . . it makes me breathless just thinking about it!" She laughed a little—a private laugh, hermetically sealed. "But why waste time thinking! Come on! Come on in!"

Laura lingered on the patio. "I'll wait out here," she said.

"Nothing of the kind," said Stephen, sternly. He admonished her as he might have admonished an undergraduate—thinly, without hope. But Laura was not an undergraduate, and she loved him, so she followed him inside.

CRAZY WATER

Margot had dived into one or another of those rooms of dark mystery. Laura and Stephen, lingering in the kitchen (one humbly, one fearfully) heard shuffling and scraping, the occasional muffled "Aha!" Laura imagined that corpses were being dragged across the floor in there; Stephen, that piles of books were shifted to make room for the viewing of a masterpiece. They inhaled the pungent stench of rotting apples, of cornucopia gone to seed.

"There! There we go! Steve! Lauren! Where are you?"

The voice summoned, and they obeyed.

"Okay! Now close your eyes!"

They squinched shut their lids, and hung hand in hand upon the threshold of who-knew-what; then Margot switched on the light, their eyes popped open, and their mutual imaginings evaporated inscrutably toward the ceiling.

"Why, Margot," Laura said.

"Well," said Stephen.

The room was filled with clothes. More than filled: it was packed, crammed, stacked. The roomness of the room was obliterated by a riot of sleeves and hems, cuffs and collars, buttons, buttons, buttons—the walls had disappeared; the horizon, it seemed, was made of silks and cottons. The clothes were not hung, but rose around them in disorganized mounds. Laura thought she saw the mounds contract and expand, inhale and exhale . . .

"Why, Margot," she said again. "This is just amazing. Really. Thank you for showing it to us."

Gripping Stephen's arm, she turned as if to go. But Stephen didn't move—his arm opposed her, and she couldn't let it go, so she stayed.

"This is nothing, dear," said Margot, modestly. "Just one room. But my favorite room. These are my favorite things . . ." She dawdled off into a corner, nearly disappearing between the clothes, and then draped a sleeve over her shoulder. "And you know what that means, Lauren. These are the newest. I always like my newest acquisitions best, don't you?"

She continued on to another mound, unearthed a silk blouse, and displayed it against herself like a jewel. "I bought all of these on my last trip. This one came from Thailand . . . they have wonderful silks there, you know, and so inexpensive . . ."

She abandoned the blouse for a fur coat—leaned into the fur as if it were a bath. "Isn't this one gorgeous? I bought it in Russia—it's easy with American dollars, and I have lots of those, you know. It's wolf."

Laura imagined Margot in Russia, pursuing wolf. But Margot had already moved on; she was ferreting something out from the bottom of a stack—the whole thing swayed, Laura and Stephen held their breath, waiting for the collapse . . . and then Margot emerged with fists full of men's shirts.

"I bought these for Harry in Bangkok. Specially cut for his measurements. He's never worn them. Imagine the waste! Cut specially for him! Nothing to be done. But now you, Steve, they might fit. Let's see if they fit."

"No, really, I couldn't," said Stephen, blushing.

"Nonsense!" said Margot. She held a shirt up against Stephen's chest, stretched the sleeves out along his arms. "Haha!" she pronounced triumphantly. "Just as I thought. They'll fit like a charm. Take them, please. I insist. They're wasted here, Steve."

"Well," Stephen said, and relented.

Laura scowled. Margot mistook her look for something else.

"Now don't think I've forgotten you, dear. Come right over here and pick something out. Anything you want."

"No thank you," Laura said. It was not the first time she had said those words to Margot, and Margot remembered.

"No thank you, no thank you, no thank you. Can't you say anything else? Honestly, Lauren, you remind me of my husband. Always saying no. Say yes for a change, dear. You'll look lovely at the faculty Christmas party in this." She held out a lavender dress with a huge ruffle at the collar and another on the rear.

Laura relinquished Stephen's arm. She left, almost before Stephen knew she meant to leave. They heard the patio door slam behind her.

"Oh dear," Margot said, absentmindedly. "Now I've offended her, haven't I?"

Stephen supposed that she had.

"Life can be so draining, Steve. University life especially. There's always someone ready to be offended. Ah well. At least there's still you and me. Let's dress for dinner, shall we?"

Stephen thought there was something wrong about it, but without Laura there to tell him, he wasn't sure just what. Besides, Laura had left without him. She'd left him there, in that closet, with Margot and Margot's clothes.

Margot took his confusion for acquiescence.

"I think we'll be eating oriental," she mused. "Let me pick out something appropriate . . ."

She wandered among the quivering soft mounds, poking here and there, sometimes leaning down so that she disappeared altogether, leaving Stephen to look longingly over his shoulder for Laura . . . Laura who was gone, Laura who had left him. Instead of Laura he found Margot offering him a blue silken kimono with a huge orange sun emblazoned on the back. And since Laura wasn't there to tell him what to do, Stephen put it on.

Margot clapped and hooted. "Perfect! Perfect! You're so perfect I could eat *you* for dinner! Now Harry, y'know, would never wear that—after all the trouble I took to get it . . . But enough, enough. Now for me . . ."

She truffled away among her acquisitions. Stephen saw stacks swaying, assumed that Margot was changing her clothes, and looked modestly at his feet. His formal shoes looked odd poking out beneath the kimono, very odd indeed, especially with that mud all over them. Suddenly inspired, he pulled off his shoes; but then his black socks looked very strange protruding beneath the blue silk, and so he took those off too. He stood in his bare feet, and felt grime beneath his toes.

Margot sashayed before him in a flowing purple sari. "What do you think, Steve? Isn't it simply de-*light*ful?"

"Delightful," Stephen echoed.

"I'm not sure," Margot said, pensive. "Maybe yellow would be more appropriate. Yes, yellow. Cheery good fellowship. Fun in the sun. Buttercups. Yellow, Steve, yellow it is!"

She disappeared again among her magical swaying piles; again the sounds of rooting and grunting;

then Margot, once again before him, this time all in yellow, like an enthusiastic summer squash.

"Now," she said, reaching out to take his hand in her jeweled pudgy one, "*we're set.*"

Stephen felt like there was something wrong about it; but since Laura wasn't there to tell him (he looked again over his shoulder, but Laura was gone), he took Margot's hand. After all, she *was* the President's Wife.

It was a mistake. For Margot, wasting no time, grasped Stephen's hand, pulled him toward her, and kissed him full on the lips.

"I knew you were different, Steve," she whispered ecstatically. "Not like Harry. Not like that idiot Drake, or that Edmondson, or Eliot Lexington. Now that *she's* gone we can be honest with each other."

Dimly (for everything became dim to Stephen as he bent, once again, to meet Margot's wrinkled old lips) it seemed to Stephen that Drake and Edmondson and Eliot Lexington were all colleagues.

"Isn't Eliot Lexington in Biology?"

Margot gave a derogatory snicker, a hoot of derision. "Yes, Steve, he's in Biology, but he's not *into* biology, if you know what I mean."

She kissed him again; Stephen knew, without Laura's advice, that he had made a mistake—but to fix it, to fix it, how would he do that?

"Margot," he sputtered, between sloppy wet ones, "you're *the President's Wife!*" He stepped backwards, his feet were caught in an invisible sleeve, and he fell. Stacks and mounds and groves of clothing fell under him, on him, and around him. He was up to his neck in textiles. Women and children had labored in sweat shops to break his fall. But as Margot had gone down with him, it seemed his metaphysical fall would continue.

"Don't let it bother you, Steve," she gasped, spitting out a shirttail. "He doesn't care. Harry doesn't care. He'll never know, Steve. This is between you and me!"

She had rolled over onto his chest and pinned him to a stack of woolens. So close, she was revolting: pockmarked face caked with makeup, hair brassily stripped and dyed. She was a pumpkin with a lascivious Halloween grin: Trick or Treat!

"You know, Steve, I always knew you were different," the pumpkin said. "From the first minute I saw you, over there at old Harrison's party—my God, what an old fart that Harrison is! Don't you think so, Steve? There are so many farts on the faculty Steve, and my Harry, the head of it all . . . Anyway, Steve, the point is, I knew it even then: *me for you, and you for me* . . ." Margot trilled to the tune of an old ballad, and her hand descended, descended through mufflers and wraps.

Stephen tried desperately to think of a literary precedent, but nothing in the canon had prepared him for Margot. All at once he was shouting: "Get off! Get off! My chest!"

"What is it, Steve?" Margot shouted back. "Is it your heart? Oh Steve! You're too young! You're too young!"

She rolled away into the piles of clothes, weeping; Stephen rolled in the opposite direction. He couldn't find his footing in that profusion of textiles; every time he thought he'd found the floor, sleeves and skirts and pant legs seemed to rise up and pull him back down. He was flailing, he knew it, but he couldn't help it; so he flailed. Clothes fell in sheets. It was a monsoon of clothes. His legs were caught in a sweater vest, his arms wrapped in a burnoose; a pair of frilly pink panties fell onto his face like a web. He kicked and spat and struggled to get free. Somewhere in that dark night of lingerie, he knew, Margot was flailing, too; although he couldn't see her he could hear her grunting, could imagine her rolling like a pumpkin, knocking down more clothing, and more, and more. All he could do was roll, desperately, away. He sank into piles of winter coats, felt mittens claim his feet, a hat with a tassel somehow lodged under his kimono; then he rolled through a springtime of blouses with ruffles, flowered aprons, and polyester stretch pants. After what seemed like months a purple bikini top attached itself to his arm, and then, all too quickly, he was back into the sweaters—itchy woolens, cotton-polyester blends, velours softer than his dead mother's hands.

Then, somehow, he was on the floor. Somehow he'd rolled off the stack and struck bottom. He peeled away layers of brassieres, underslips, and nighties. Margot had stopped flailing too and was curled in her robe atop a heap of cashmere sweaters, face hidden in her hands. From behind the hands emanated a sound like crying.

"I think," Stephen said, "there's been a misunderstanding."

And taking up his shoes, he left.

While he had been flailing in the seas of haute couture it had turned to dusk, then dark. Amazing, Stephen thought, stepping through grass and crickets, how it all continued without him. In the morning he had set out in his car with his wife; now he had neither, and had to walk, alone. Down the driveway he went, still carrying his shoes. Margot's house receded behind him until, with its few lights burning, it came to resemble a ship, unanchored, floating up and away into the inky sky.

At the bottom of the driveway his car was parked; his wife was in it, sleeping, with a map over her face.

"At last, Amerigo," she mumbled, and moved aside to let him behind the steering wheel. She didn't mention his bare feet, or his kimono.

Stephen started up the car and they pulled out onto the dark country road.

"I think this is the way," he said.

But in a few minutes they knew that they were more lost than ever.

. . .

Romulus

*S*omething's wrong, she said to him. With the children, she said. Yours, she said, and mine. Very wrong.

What did he do? He rattled the newspaper. He always held the newspaper with the business pages facing out. He rattled it and moved his feet a little bit. Moved his feet in those brown slippers, while sitting in his brown chair.

So she went away. Went into another room, perhaps, where she could walk back and forth, stopping only to pick things up, pausing only to put them down.

She could hear him in the next room, rattling his newspaper.

She walked around, picking things up and putting them down. She smoothed her fingers over small objects made from glass. She waited for a sound from the children's rooms.

•

Look how perfect he is! So cunning, perched on his haunches. So alert. He looks swiftly from side to side, wriggling his nose, prepared to leap away at the slightest sign of danger. I admire him as I admire all perfection, and now, when he looks at me in return, his eyes are filled with affection. Look! He jumps up when I clap my hands.

I began teaching him that long ago. I started by throwing up a bit of candy in the air, clapping my hands at the same time. At first he jumped for the candy. Now he jumps just for me.

He runs! Off he goes, through the hedge. Beyond a doubt, she has rung the dinner bell.

The hedges sway in his wake. I go out back, and adjust the sprinkler.

Don't you love to listen to the sprinkler on a hot summer day? It spits against the back of the house just the way that I did, when I was a boy.

•

Then there's the other child, Katie. A lovely little girl. She has long, long black hair, and eyes the color of pine trees. She won't come through the hedge, not yet. Instead she stands there and looks at me through the little leaves and branches. What a beauty! I'd like to tear down my own hedge, just to get a better look at Katie.

•

She didn't know what to do. That was because he wouldn't answer her, ever. Instead he acted as though they weren't his children at all. Suddenly it had become one of those marriages, where everything concerning the children was left to the wife. Or maybe it wasn't so sudden. Maybe instead it happened slowly. She said to him, Dearest, something is wrong with the children. With our son Evan. With our daughter Katie. And he replied, Nonsense my dear. Our children are fine. Beautiful. Healthy. With black hair and green eyes. Leave them alone.

So she went through the rooms, picking things up, then putting them down. Adjusting the curtains. Trying not to hear the noises from the children's rooms.

They were nice curtains. Lace and puffy ruffles, in some rooms white, in some yellow, in others brown. When she pushed the curtains aside, the bright outdoors was always a surprise. Sometimes she could see the children in the yard, playing.

She would quickly pull the curtains. That way she didn't have to see the children again, until it was time to ring the dinner bell.

•

You can tell she doesn't understand it. I see her sometimes, standing at the window, looking out. No! She doesn't understand it at all. Just the same she looks like the little girl. Long black hair. Eyes from the forest. In the morning she steps outside to kiss her husband goodbye. She stands on the back porch. Goodbye Goodbye! she waves, as he drives away. Very early in the morning. Just about the time when I set the sprinkler out in the yard.

•

And this is what the neighborhood looks like: very ordinary. Cute little houses, two storey, one storey, bushes and stuff out front, nice colors, sedate and suburban. White, yellow, brown, an occasional grey or maroon. The lawns are green and sparkly from water spat by sprinklers. Here and there, white wooden fences, prickly green hedges. Swing sets and swimming pools that can be glimpsed from the street.

Plenty of trees. There's no lack of shade, in this particular neighborhood. In spite of the summer sun, lots of deep shady places you could disappear into through a gap in a fence. Perfect for children.

A safe convenient neighborhood, in that sense.

•

I say these things smugly, as if I understand them, myself.

At least I try to understand. I clap my hands and he jumps up in the air, laughing.

Soon I will teach him other things, too.

Soon his lovely sister Katie will dare to walk through my hedge.

•

Nothing she could do would convince him that something was wrong. He wasn't home much, that was the real problem. He never got to see the things that were wrong, only saw that his wife wasn't as attentive to the children as he thought she should have been. She seemed to be wandering around the house a lot, dusting and so forth, smoothing the couch covers, but never going near the children, or talking to them. He was concerned about it, but he never thought the problem was with the children.

He even spoke about it with his neighbor once, over the hedge.

It's my wife, he said. I get the feeling she doesn't like the children. She doesn't talk to them. She won't look at them. What can I do? They're perfect children.

The neighbor was sympathetic. Maybe if you were to discuss it with her, the neighbor suggested. After all, she's new to motherhood.

This cheered the husband up. He let his neighbor go back to adjusting the sprinkler.

Only when he had gone back into the house did it occur to him that his wife had been mother to the girl for ten years, and to the boy for six.

·

It began, she thought, when Evan was the right age to walk and talk. She noticed right away that he didn't show as much interest in those things as other children do. The little girl with the black hair, who everyone said looked so much like her mother, had been precocious. So precocious that she had seemed to become an adult at a very young age.

But Evan would not walk or talk. She spent hours by his bed and his high chair, reading, talking, singing. She led him around by the hands on the living room rug. But Evan only stared at her. It wasn't that he seemed dumb. On the contrary, he was always alert. Sometimes she even thought he smiled, but they were such strange smiles that she could never be sure.

And the minute she released his hands, he would

drop down on the carpet and twist his head from side to side. Then he would race back to his room, always on his hands and knees.

When he twisted his head like that, she started to feel that he was laughing at her. It was only a matter of time before she stopped trying to teach Evan to walk and talk, just because she couldn't stand that feeling, that he was laughing.

•

She pushed the white curtains aside and looked out at the children, playing in the back yard. What beautiful children! She had never seen such black hair, such green eyes. Evan lay on his belly in the grass, surrounded by dandelions. He was looking up at his sister. She stood right in front of him, holding out her hands. Then she clapped, and Evan leapt up in the air!

He rolled on his back in the grass. Katie rolled with him, tickling his stomach.

From behind the closed window, their mother could hear them laughing, and then she let the curtain fall.

•

And then the husband complained to his neighbor: I know my wife has no interest in our children. Imagine! She even sets my son's dinner dish on the floor. Fills it with food, sets it on the floor, and then rings the dinner bell.

•

At first I only wanted to watch them. They were always interesting to watch, because they were so beautiful. I would go out in the back yard during my free time, sit around on a lawn chair, always placed just so I could look through the hedge. How could I help but admire their perfection? Then sometimes the boy would yowl, and roll in the grass, and try to bite his sister's fingers. At other times he was quiet, staring at the back of the house.

If I looked that way myself, quickly enough, I'd see the mother, my next door neighbor, hiding herself behind a curtain, at one window or another.

I'd been at their house before, right after they first moved in. The children were smaller then. I carried over a plateful of something, the woman opened the door, Hello, hello, new neighbors, welcome. I commented on the children right away, after all, I'd noticed them the first.

What a beautiful daughter, I said. What a handsome son. I'm not married. No children, myself.

Right away the woman took the plate out of my hands and disappeared into another room, but the husband was pleased, he huffed and puffed and smiled a lot, gazed paternally at the children where they were playing on the rug, picked me out immediately as a friend. He wanted me to go out back and discuss the best ways to keep the lawn green. I'm always obliging, of course, I was all set to follow him, but not without first getting closer to the children. I had a little piece of candy hidden in my palm, and I slipped it to the boy as I followed his father.

That was how I began, that was the first piece of candy.

•

So I wasn't surprised when the children stood at my hedge. The boy was on his hands and knees, as usual, and not afraid at all. He poked his head right through the branches and stared at me, wriggling his nose. The girl was behind him, looking, coming no closer. That was as close as she would ever come.

•

The husband confides in me sometimes. He'll come over to the hedge with something, pruning shears maybe, it always has to be in the context of yard work for him. Then he says, My wife hates our children, she thinks my son is strange, can you imagine, his own mother.

Then he says other things: She thinks something's wrong, she demands I do something about it, but what am I supposed to do, as far as I'm concerned the boy is fine, she wants to take him somewhere but as far as I'm concerned it's a waste of time.

Since it's what he wants, I give him comforting words: You know how women are, it isn't easy to stay home with children all day, try to give her some understanding, all children go through these phases.

And so forth.

I say these things smugly, as if I understand them.

•

Since he was unable to listen to her, she took her son to the doctor without bothering to tell her husband. The doctor sat the boy on a metal table, stripped him down to his underwear, looked in his ears and up his nose, tapped his back, listened to his heart, and told her that her son was healthy.

Yes doctor, she said, he's healthy, but the thing is, doctor, my boy Evan thinks he's a dog. He won't walk, doctor, or talk, only crawls and barks. He won't eat his dinner unless I set it on the floor, just like I would for a dog. His sister teaches him tricks . . .

The doctor lifted Evan down from the examining table and tried to make him stand, but Evan collapsed down onto his hands, then gritted his teeth and backed away from the doctor, just like an animal.

And so the doctor sent Evan to have certain tests. Electrodes were pasted on his scalp. Evan squirmed and howled; his mother clutched her purse. Lights flashed on and off in Evan's face.

The woman took her son home to wait. She spent the rest of the afternoon washing the paste out of his hair, so that her husband would never know.

·

Otherwise he was a good father. He kept the lawn trim, he was good at fixing things around the house. He liked his time to himself, though. They could be in a room together and yet just the same she would be alone. It was the way he acted: picking up the newspaper, scuffing his slippers on the rug, not meeting her eyes. When he was like that she felt the most alone of all. She would sit in the room with him, and then when she couldn't stand it anymore she'd go out into the rest of the house. All summer the house was dark and humid with silence, for she kept the windows shut, the curtains pulled. She said it was to keep out the sun. She would wander from one darkened room to the next, always knowing where she would end up but pretending to avoid it anyway, by adjusting a pillow or straightening an ashtray. But then she would be in the hallway outside her daughter's room, in spite of herself her ear would be pressed to the smooth white door, she'd hear Evan and Katie whispering together; sometimes they talked loudly; they laughed often.

She couldn't understand what they said. Only Evan and Katie could understand it, she knew that, although she couldn't tell her husband. All she understood was the laughter.

•

Look! He sits up and begs, waving his hands in the air like little white paws. He's quite beautiful, the black hair, the alert face. At a word from me he flops over onto the grass and lies perfectly still; he won't even move when a spider tiptoes across his face. He'll lie in the grass like that all day, evening will come to bruise the sky, then night with clouds of moths fluttering around my porch light, still he'll stay right there, without moving. He'll stay until I clap my hands, and then he jumps up, I reward him with candy and we laugh together, the boy and I and his sister, who stands watching through the gap in the hedge.

•

I've noticed they have their own secret ways. There are certain days when I don't see them, although I stay outside for hours, waiting. I say to myself: perhaps they're in the house today; but I know they aren't; I look at the house and see their mother hiding behind the curtains, at one window and then another, and then surely at other windows beyond my line of vision. She's looking for them, too.

•

It's a nice neighborhood. Convenient, safe, with those typical suburban houses, Cape style, ranch, split level, all painted conservative colors. Yet there are still plenty of places to go, missing slats in a fence creating gaps that lead to secret places, filled with trees and moss and squat mushrooms. Or holes in hedges that lead to completely different worlds.

•

He went to his neighbor's house and said, I have a bad feeling, my wife is behaving strangely, she refuses to confide in me. What can I do?

For the first time his neighbor didn't have much to say, only sat in a wing-backed chair and smoked. Suddenly the husband realized he'd never been inside his neighbor's house before. In fact he'd never been invited, but he wasn't the type to back down because of that. Instead he walked around the living room a little bit, looking at things. There were framed photos hanging on the walls, and in each one he saw young versions of his neighbor, smiling and posing always with a black German shepherd, holding up a trophy or a ribbon. He knew it couldn't be the same dog in every photo but just the same they all looked alike, each dog identical to the one before.

Well, said the husband, drawn out of his own thoughts for a minute because he'd never known anything about his neighbor's past before, did you raise them yourself or just train?

The neighbor smiled at that, he seemed pleased. Both, he said, but in the end it became too expensive, I had to give it up. I loved it while it lasted. I could train my dogs to do anything, anything at all.

Oh, that's nice, said the husband. A nice hobby for a man who doesn't have a family.

Indeed, said the neighbor, and smoked a little more.

The husband went home, and there was a feeling of uneasiness in him that didn't fade until he left for work the next morning.

•

I saw them disappear once myself, through a gap in the back fence. The girl went first, looking around, looking especially at the house. Then she turned herself sideways and squeezed through in a place where some boards had fallen out. Her brother, without even bothering to look around, leaped into the gash of green right on her heels.

•

She goes from one window to another, upstairs and downstairs. I see the curtains move. They part slowly and her face appears in the dark slit. She watches the children, never saying anything to them, never opening a window or calling out. She has seen them come to my hedge; she looks in the direction of my yard even when they aren't there. She watches me in the morning when I set out the sprinkler. But if I happen to catch her eye, immediately the curtain falls, the house goes back to stillness.

•

Each time, his sister comes a little closer. I can see the beads of sweat on her forehead, the bits of grass in her hair. As soon as I smile and gesture she steps back, but I know she can hear the sprinkler hissing in my yard and so I say, You look so hot, Katie, why don't you come and cool off under the sprinkler? She bites her lip and looks down at the ground, and Evan becomes jealous, he yips and grabs the leg of my trousers in his teeth. I hold the piece of candy up high, dangle it between my fingers.

Evan yowls and rolls his eyes. For the first time, I hold the candy higher than he can jump, and he begs until I laugh. I laugh so much that tears run down my face. When I suddenly look back at the hedge, I see Katie retreating. She runs, barefooted, in the direction of home.

•

She noticed that they didn't always stay in the yard. She would look out and not be able to find them. To distract herself from it she wandered around the house, dusting here or there, but inevitably she was drawn to another window, thinking, Maybe they're on this side of the house after all.

Yet when she rang the dinner bell they would appear at the back door, laughing, covered with dirt, with twigs and leaves in their hair.

Each time, she felt that they must be laughing at her.

•

She watched her son play. He rolled a red ball across the living room floor. He lay on his stomach and pushed the ball back and forth, from one hand to the other.

Sometimes, he stopped the ball with his nose, then tried to grab it with his teeth.

Put that down, Evan, she said. Down. Put it down.

Evan held the ball in his mouth. He looked at her, tilting his head to one side.

Put it down, Evan, she said.

When he tilted his head like that, she felt that he was laughing at her. Her daughter Katie was sitting in the den, reading a book.

Katie smiled at her.

She heard Evan barking. He had pushed his ball into the hallway, chasing it on his hands and knees, and Katie smiled at that.

She left the house. It was hotter outside than she realized.

•

Finally he stands up. Stands up to take the candy from my hand! He doesn't like it much, his legs wobble, he rolls his eyes and grits his teeth, but he stands. His sister Katie isn't by the hedge anymore. The minute he stands, she runs away. I see her black hair whip behind her as she runs.

•

A neighborhood where children grow up normal. Normal, yes, that's it. Not even the teeth are crooked. A neighborhood where a woman feels funny, walking down the street, if her children aren't as good as everyone else's. She feels very funny, walking down the street in the hot summer sun.

•

She had never been inside her neighbor's house, but she felt the need to go somewhere, since her husband refused to listen. Of course she hadn't gone out with that intention, she'd just begun to walk, and there was her neighbor out in his front yard, clipping the little bushes he'd planted along the house. He waved and smiled, and although she'd never liked him, really, she felt the need to speak. Hello, how are you, hot enough for you? That kind of thing. So when he invited her to come in and visit for a minute, it seemed like the right thing to do. She sat in his wing-backed chair, he brought her a glass of iced tea, she looked around at the pictures on the wall, then she looked right at him.

You know, she said, my son is sick, although the doctor tells me he's healthy. He constantly acts like an animal. No one can talk to him except his sister. My husband refuses to admit anything is wrong.

She looked down at the glass in her hand.

•

She's got that blue-black hair just like her daughter, and the same uneasy look, like a bird, ready to fly off at any minute. She glances around restlessly, her eyes never meet mine.

Finally I tell her, I was able to train my dogs to do anything. Anything at all.

She looks at me at last, lifting her eyes from the glass of iced tea.

Anything, I tell her. I could train them to do anything.

•

Evan rolled on his back, in the dandelions. His sister stood above him. She held the edges of her skirt in her hands and began to twirl around and around. Right away Evan jumped up and circled her, barking. He circled closer and closer, until finally they both fell in the grass in a heap, laughing.

Their mother dropped the curtain and turned inward, to the house.

•

He hates to stand this way, his legs shake so much, his hands wave helplessly up and down, he seems embarrassed almost, and relieved when I finally relent and give him the piece of candy. His sister calls to him, using words I can't understand. But he ignores her and gazes up at me, his eyes full of affection, until she stomps her feet and rattles the hedge with anger.

I hold up a second piece of candy and he stands again, I begin to walk away, always dangling that bit of candy. Evan takes a step toward me and his sister cries out, some angry word that makes Evan drop down on his hands again.

I shrug my shoulders at him. Then I walk away. I go into my house. I shut the door.

Evan stays in the back yard, staring after me, until his mother rings the dinner bell.

•

One day I see her husband in the street, walking past my house, so I wave to him and call his name. He hasn't come to see me for several days. I ask, How is it between you and your wife, things must be better since you haven't needed to talk lately.

He gives me a funny look, as if he doesn't know what to say, but finally he realizes that he must speak. Well, he says, she's quiet now, she doesn't complain much, but she has this smug look all the time, it really makes me nervous. I'm sure she's done something, I just don't know what it might be.

Whatever it is, I assure him, no doubt it will be for the best.

He nods and walks off very quickly, without saying goodbye, headed away from his home.

•

For the first time, she had set his place at the table. Katie and her husband watched, without speaking. Evan sat perfectly still, perfectly polite, while she hovered around the kitchen, filling glasses, arranging plates. Then she set his food in front of him. Evan stared at his dish and around at his family. He lowered his face into the food, and began to eat.

Katie clapped joyfully.

Excuse me, said her husband, and left the table.

•

When he stands he is like a dog trained to be a boy. His steps are slow, disjointed, he holds his arms slightly raised and bent at the wrists, his head leans toward one shoulder. I throw him his piece of candy, and he sits down in my lawn chair, wriggling a little, just the way any other boy would.

Remarkable! To be so perfect, so alert, so intelligent. Although his sister cries out objections through the hedge, I place various objects in his hands: combs, silverware, shoelaces.

When his mother rings the dinner bell he walks

haltingly, parting my hedge with his awkward hands. Katie will not wait for him. When he comes to her, she runs away.

•

She opened the window. Evan was in the back yard. He kicked a ball against the side of the house.

She didn't see Katie. She went from one window to the next, but she didn't see Katie anywhere. She didn't notice when Evan stopped kicking the ball, and instead began to roll in the grass.

•

He will do anything at all, for the sake of the candy I hide in my palm. He will lie in the grass through nights and days without moving. He will push toy trucks, set tables, serve glasses of water, tie his own shoelaces, tie mine.

Katie will only watch, silently, from the other side of my hedge.

•

He was disturbed by it all, frankly, he didn't like it, although it was true that Evan acted more like a boy than a dog. He was uneasy, because of the smug look his wife had, and the smug look his neighbor had.

Romulus

And then one night his neighbor came to dinner and said, You know, Evan's quite a bright boy, he can do anything, with the right motivation, and the neighbor clapped his hands, and Evan jumped up from the chair where he'd been sitting and filled all the glasses on the table with water.

I've had him working on another project too, said the neighbor, for your amusement. He clapped his hands and Evan shuffled across the kitchen floor to a beat pounded out by the tip of his neighbor's spoon.

His wife looked smug, she clapped and laughed. She and the neighbor laughed together, and then the neighbor lit a cigarette and said, You must admit, Evan's been improving quite a bit lately.

Yes, the husband admitted it, Evan had been acting more like a boy of his age.

His wife and his neighbor laughed more.

He was so disturbed by it all that he ate in silence, and then went into the other room, to read the newspaper.

His wife came into the room and said, Have you seen the children? I can't find them anywhere.

She said she had gone from window to window, and hadn't been able to find them.

No, he said, I haven't seen the children since dinner.

Well, she said, what if you were to get up, for a change, and go out, for a change, and look?

And so he got up, and went outside.

•

It was a nice neighborhood, in that sense. Safe, convenient, with plenty of places to hide. A neighborhood designed for children, filled with places to hide.

•

They had gone through the gap in the fence. He followed them out into the summer dusk, carrying a flashlight, calling their names: Evan, Katie, Katie, Evan. He followed the edges of the yard, poking at bushes, peering behind trees, until he saw Evan's shoes lying by the back fence. He knew there was a vacant lot behind the fence, he remembered that as a child he had liked to play in vacant lots, and so he thought nothing of going over the fence after them. He could already hear their voices, he only had to step through some tall grass, and part some branches, and he could see them. Katie sat primly on the ground. Evan lay on the grass beside her, his face smeared with dirt, growling deep in his throat, chewing on the edge of her dress. She talked to her brother softly, in a language their father could not understand.

He stood for a while behind a tree. When he looked back toward his house he could see that the lights were on. He knew that his wife was moving from window to window, room to room, watching.

· · ·

Mother-in-Law

*M*uch to our dismay, she's moved in right beneath us: Mother-in-Law, jingling like a dime beneath our feet. All night long we can hear her through the floorboards: *jingle, jingle, jingle,*—"that's Mother-in-Law," we say, "unpacking her twelve scarlet suitcases with their twelve silver buckles, her thirteen tiny hatboxes with their clasps of precious metal." We see that she's brought her aquarium and hyacinths in pots and seventy-five balls of yarn—all the colors of spring, enough to knit a Matisse that would cover us three and our apartments and the stairwell in between them and all of our furniture and maybe the balcony as well.

"It looks," I tell my husband, "like she means to stay."

My husband's broken up about it; after all, she's my Mother-in-Law, but she's his mother; there he is, right in the middle, between her fearsome knitting needles and my monumental, yawning discontent (I've been yawning like a tiger ever since she moved in—can't help it, can't help that reek of blood and revenge around my molars, it's Mother-in-Law after all, downstairs, right beneath me, *in the same building*, and all that infernal jingling, all night long. I never sleep anymore).

My husband is a good son. "Mother's looking rather thin," he says, with a worried face, and I have to admit it's true; Mother-in-Law looked gaunt to me on the morning that she dragged those suitcases up the stairs—haggard. "The runes of death around her eyes," I thought, peering down at her from the landing as she hauled those jingling suitcases, one after the other, determined as an ant. (But I wouldn't help Mother-in-Law; no, I'm pretending I can't see her, I'm blind to her, as far as she can tell I don't know that she exists. "I don't want you kids to pay any attention to me," she had said, over the telephone, before she came; as far as she knows, I'm taking her at her word.)

"I think we should invite Mother up for dinner," my husband says.

I feel sorry for my husband. All day long he works at a job he doesn't like. He wears a necktie, phones ring all around him, editors dart in and out with fury in their faces and death in their eyes, lunch is a grilled cheese sandwich in a diner—and now look what he's got, a wife with a carnivorous smile and there, downstairs, right there beneath his feet—his *mother*.

I give in for other reasons, as well. After all, I like our life. Every morning when I rise (late, and with the shadows of jingling beneath my eyes), I step out onto the balcony with a glass in my hand, and feel like I'm soaring among the treetops. I feel like our balcony is a mesa in a jungle, and here I am, eye to eye with the butterflies, surrounded by nothing but the green whispering of the trees. I can sit for hours, with a glass in my hand, and imagine that I'm all alone, listening to birdsong in the jungle. I'd bitterly hate to give it all up, just because of my Mother-in-Law.

So I invite her.

She comes to dinner in a scarlet dress, carrying a tissue to wipe her eye. I notice for the first time that Mother-in-Law has a cataract. Her eye has grown cloudy, opaque; it weeps against her volition (she wept at our wedding, too, but that was a different matter; her eyes were clear then, very clear). She brings a bottle of Chianti, some slippers she's knitted in purple and blue, and an album filled with photos of last summer's trip to Italy. She says she hated Venice: there was garbage floating in the canals.

"Flies everywhere!" she exclaims, sniffing and weeping as if she could smell it still.

Right then, almost against my will, I begin to feel sorry for Mother-in-Law. I think, "Mother-in-Law is lonely." I think, "Mother-in-Law is alone." I think, "Mother-in-Law has come here because she is lonely and alone."

I propose a toast to her health, and we sip Chianti on the balcony, watching moths that flutter like pale hands around the floodlights. Crickets are chirping; and very far away, beyond the trees, we can hear cars pass on the motorway. Mother-in-Law looks at my husband and gives a gentle sigh.

"It would be so nice to be a young mother again," she says. She smiles, and the opaque eye glitters crazily in the dim light.

"Mother-in-Law is pathetic," I think, "sad. Mother-in-Law is deserving of pity." My attitude toward Mother-in-Law changes. She needs a friend; I will be that friend. I imagine us together, sitting on the balcony (sipping, sipping), binoculars clasped tight to our eyes, trying to identify species of jungle birds; I imagine us in the department store, trying on floral swimsuits together (the image is so vivid I can *actually smell the latex!*); I imagine long girlish chats late into the night. She will tell me what it was like to give birth to my husband: how it hurt her, tore her, but how it was worth it after all. She will tell me how pungent it was, his first shit. How happy they were about it: "We thought there was something wrong! He didn't shit for days!" But it opened the floodgate: all those diapers! She will tell me his first words. Through the memory of Mother-in-Law, I will watch my husband grow up again.

Everything's grown dim with love and Chianti; I'm longing to hug Mother-in-Law, and so I do. In surprise she overturns her glass of wine onto my husband's shirt. We all jump up, there's a fluster of drunken *oh no*s and *I'm sorry*s and *silly me*s and *my fault entirely*s, the glowing white moths that have been resting secretly on our legs flutter toward heaven, someone drops a cushion onto the carpet, someone else says *I think we'd better go to bed now.* We stumble back into the apartment, leaning on each other's shoulders, and say goodnight in a spirit of fond good fellowship; Mother-in-Law plucks her photo album off the couch and stumbles down the stairs, looking frail and innocent in the florescent glow of the landing lights. She waves at me with the crumpled, tear-stained tissue she's been clutching all night; I lean over the landing, watching as she dabs at her milky eye, then disappears into the apartment beneath ours.

My husband is in the bathroom, trying to rinse

the scarlet stain off the sleeve of his new white shirt. His face is anguished, like a little boy's. "It's ruined!" he says. "She ruined it! That's just like my mother!"

The nape of his neck looks so tender as he leans over the sink, rinsing and rinsing the stained shirt under the hot tap, then the cold, then the hot again. He doesn't say anything, but he's pleased that I hugged his mother; I'm sure of it.

In the morning, everything looks new. I go downstairs to greet my Mother-in-Law, and I find her knitting. She's sitting on a settee in the living room, surrounded by plants—not just the familiar hyacinths, but other plants as well: huge violets with great, thick green stems and faces like hungry stars, luxuriant petunias lined with red and black, orchids that crouch like leopards along the walls. Whatever she's knitting is pearly grey; it spills off her lap and disappears into the lush green underbrush.

I'm curious, but I don't ask; instead, I look around for a place to set down the tray I've brought her (Mother-in-Law looks so thin; I've brought her toast with eggs for breakfast). But everything is covered with green, or with pearly grey; there's no room for breakfast.

"Oh, just set it down anywhere!" Mother-in-Law laughs, tinkling like a wind chime. "Yes, yes, right there, on the floor, that's just fine!"

Mother-in-Law

I set the toast and eggs down among the stems and branches. Mother-in-Law wipes her weepy eye.

"It's such a dreadful habit I have," she says, apologetically, "this knitting. Once I pick it up, I just can't put it down. I started when I was expecting John," she says. "Yes, that's when I started. Now I'm doing it again." She laughs a little; it's a self-deprecating laugh, I think.

I invite Mother-in-Law to come upstairs for lunch. "We can watch the birds," I say, tapping my binoculars (I wear them all the time, from the moment I get up in the morning until I go to sleep at night. Once I fell asleep with the binoculars on; they weighed on my chest like death). "We can drink some wine."

Mother-in-Law sits on her settee, knitting. "Oh, why, thank you, dear," she says, "but I don't want to disrupt your day. Just forget I'm here, really." She smiles serenely, surrounded by green and grey, and I think: *she's the Madonna of the bushes.*

Her refusal makes me angry; I can't deny it. I drop the binoculars onto my chest with a thud. "Fine," I say. "That's all right, Mother. You can't say I didn't try." I turn on my heel; my back is as stiff and as brittle as a wand of coral. I peek over my shoulder (a subtle peek, too subtle for Mother-in-Law to notice) and I see that she's still knitting, knitting, knitting;

she doesn't even look up at me. Toast and eggs are turning cold at her feet.

I shut the door with a resounding *slam!*

Upstairs, I make myself a drink.

All day I wait for Mother-in-Law to call, to apologize, to beg my pardon. I mix one drink after another; I see Amazonian butterflies fluttering around my balcony; a quetzal is roosting in the pine tree by my bedroom window. Finally, at seven, when I've given up hope, the telephone rings; it is Mother-in-Law.

"Is John there?" she asks, sweetly. I hear a faint crumpling noise and know it must be the sound of a white tissue wiping a milky white eye.

"It's your *mother!*" I snarl, and toss my husband the phone.

They only talk for a moment; I don't hear my name. I'm at the kitchen table, identifying seashells. "It's *Zonaria annettae*," I say.

"I'll be right back," says my husband, "my mother wants me." And just like that, he disappears down the stairs.

I wait, drinking and snarling, snarling and drinking, holding *Nerita peloronta* up to the light (the better to see the bloody spot on its upper lip). I imagine my husband downstairs, among those plants, talking to his mother: talking about *me!*

"You never should have married her, John,"

Mother-in-Law

Mother-in-Law might be saying, twining her foot in a vine. "I told you once, I'm telling you again."

"Yes, Mother," John says, sitting at his mother's knee, "you're right. She's a beast."

(*I'm a hyena strolling the African plains; I'm sticking my big mangy head up over golden waves of tundra grass, I'm snuffing the air, because there, right there, is a meal under a bush: it's Mother-in-Law, wearing a pink housedress yanked up to show a little bit of yellowed bloomer, sagging stockings and grey orthopedic shoes, unlaced; she's rolled up in grey skeins of knitting, struggling to get free, bouncing her knitting needles helplessly—she's tied herself up in knots. I advance, grinning, clutching a martini in my paw, wondering: should I eat her? Should I eat my Mother-in-Law? I imagine what it would be like to take my Mother-in-Law apart, piece by piece; meaty enough in the thighs, sure, but what about those scrawny arms? Those arthritic shoulders? That wrinkled belly? The unmentionable breasts? What about that milky white eye? I imagine myself up to my chin in bloody sinews, laughing a hyena laugh up and down the plains . . .*)

I add more orange juice to my vodka, and then my husband comes in; he's dressed like a puppet, in a grey knit suit with a red lace collar and little mother-of-pearl buttons. He sits on the couch, cradling his head in his hands.

His words are brief, but eloquent. "She's trying to suck me back," he says. "Back into the womb."

I can't help it, no I can't stop myself; I'm laughing, laughing a big hyena laugh that bounds across the balcony, past Mother-in-Law's open windows, on and out into the night; it joins the cars rushing up and down the motorway, tucks itself under their axles, speeds off for points unknown.

"You're crazy," I say. I straighten his lace collar on my way to bed.

Mother-in-Law discovers a genius for knitting. If I put my ear to the floor (resting my hot cheek against the cool, smooth floorboards) I can hear the click of her knitting needles. Likewise, if I stand just outside her door—delicately, poised with care on my toes so that there is no sound, no revealing creak—I can hear the clicking, hear Mother-in-Law talking softly to herself; I can even hear the soft slither of yarn across her scarlet lap. If I happen, just by chance, to pass outside Mother-in-Law's window (pursuing, perhaps, a further glimpse of the elusive quetzal), I can see her inside, sitting in her chair with a cup of tea by her elbow, concentrating on her knitting. Skeins of blue emerge from her needles, shaped into sleeves and trouser cuffs, neckties and little hats. In the evening she comes silently to the door and hands me a package (always wrapped in innocent, crinkling brown paper); she smiles absentmindedly and turns away. There are no words between us; no apology from her, nor, as far as I can tell, any acknowledgment of my anger (which is justified: by her cruel refusal of my friendship, by her indifference to the quetzal outside our mutual windows, by her failure to knit anything for me—nothing for me in the packages, not even a knit bathing suit, not a scarf, not a glove, not a sock, nothing). The packages contain presents for my husband. She has knit entire business suits in sweet shades of pale blue; she provides everything, even a little knit hanky in the breast pocket of each jacket. My husband complains, but every day he leaves the apartment in the latest suit.

"The other guys make fun of me," he says, grimly twisting a finger between his neck and the collar of Mother-in-Law's latest knit shirt. For it's a fact that Mother-in-Law has no sense of proportion: the suits never fit. The trousers are too short, the sleeves hang just past the elbows, the collars are too narrow (luckily, they can be stretched; by inserting our fingers or even, if necessary, an entire hand, we can make the collars wider), seams and buttons are constantly popping, in short my husband makes a spectacle of himself every day, and all to please his mother. Worst of all are the funny little hats: mostly berets, but also some funny, free-form toppers with doily fringes or odd, braided tassels. In the evening my husband confides that he doesn't wear the hats: out the door, past his mother's windows, sure, just to please her, but once around the corner, he takes off the hat and shoves it somewhere, under a hedge, into a mailbox, even sometimes (when it's especially offensive, the hat) into a trash can.

"You don't have to wear the stuff, you know," I say, all in a spirit of fun—because I know my husband doesn't feel that way; on the contrary, he feels he does have to wear it. It's his duty to wear what his mother knits.

"Her feelings will get hurt," he says.

Ever since his father died, my husband's been this way about his mother: oversolicitous, I'd call it.

I do call it. "You're oversolicitous," I say, wiping my tongue around my bright, pointy teeth.

"You're just jealous," he says.

Of course, he's right: but my jealousy has so many points and corners, so many twisting avenues, so many intertwining protuberances that I'm no longer sure of whom I'm jealous, or why, or when the jealousy started.

"Well," I mutter miserably, pinning a new sample

into my display case, "she could make something for me, just once."

We glare at each other across the latest baby-blue knit jumper.

(I suppose things between us have never been what I'd call harmonious, but it was always agreeable; in spite of all the rough spots, my snarls and his yawns, our mutual suspiciousness, the occasional disagreement over rice and macaroni, there were still those moments of coming together: quiet purple dawns heralded by the cry of the quetzal, pleasant meetings of the eye and the hand between cool bedsheets and in other places as well. Now there is only jealousy, guarded eyes, the hostile wordless bumping of knees, hands that possess and hands that long to possess the manna, those magical strands purling off Mother-in-Law's rose-red lap. I disguise my avarice by collecting: butterflies, seashells, gemstones, pressed flowers, teeth spurned and abandoned. By the light of the lamp, he silently reads the newspaper.)

One day, I discover that Mother-in-Law has a social life. I come down the stairs and find a bent and

bearded man clutching a bouquet of posies just outside Mother-in-Law's door; the forefinger of his right
hand is poised just above the doorbell—he has either
rung it or will ring it, I think, smilesnarling as I pass.
He nods and winks and eyes the binoculars that lie
on my chest.

"Selling something, pal?" I ask—not out of rude-
ness, of course, but out of pure curiosity, combined
with a certain involuntary concern for Mother-in-
Law; after all, she's all alone, alone and lonely and
vulnerable, there among her plants and her knitting.
And what's more, the gent looks a bit like a salesman,
in a checked suit gone shiny at the elbows and at the
knees, and with a battered leather valise reclining at
his feet, just outside Mother-in-Law's doorway. He
could have anything in that valise, I think, picturing
horrors both traditional and untraditional (liquor,
dice, girlie magazines, somebody's stolen prosthetics,
maybe even a glass eye or a stained deck of *Go Fish*).

The gent is just beginning to reply (his open jaw
reveals a whitish tongue and a peppering of isolated
teeth) when Mother-in-Law appears at the door. She's
smiling, until she sees me; then the smile stops up,
maybe even turns into a pucker.

"Is everything okay here, Mother?" I ask, as solici-
tously as I can, perhaps with even a trace of oversolic-
itousness (I'm thinking of nice new knit sweaters and

skirts, maybe even girlish knee socks embroidered with dancing reindeer).

"Just fine, dear," Mother-in-Law says. The yellowing old gent and his tattered valise step inside with a wink, and the door slams shut in my face. I have barely enough time to glimpse the green, forested interior of Mother-in-Law's living room. Only later, when I've successfully catalogued three ibis and a hummingbird, do I realize that Mother-in-Law was wearing a pink negligee that revealed (oh immodesty!) a shadow of cleavage, her wrinkled kneecaps, and a bit of a belly.

"Your mother's getting fat," I tell my husband. He's anguished at the idea that his mother might be dating, can't believe it in fact; ever since I told him, he's been spinning his little red top around the dining room floor, making wagers with himself: *if it lands point up, she's dating; if it lands point down, she's not.*

"Look on the bright side," I say, "maybe this fella's taking her out to dinner. A nice fatty round of pork chops, potatoes baked and fried, maybe even the occasional lobster. It was you," I add, "who was worried about her weight."

But John won't be consoled; all weekend we languish in an uneasy malaise. As I wander from room to room (measuring a stone here, a seashell there, reposing a stuffed bird on a shelf, peering down with my binoculars at an especially tantalizing blossom) I can hear the little red top scrolling across the floor. At night, although we try not to listen, we can't help but hear Mother-in-Law jingling like a dime beneath our feet—and every now and then the muted sound of laughter.

On Sunday morning we happen to run into her in the hallway; she's wearing a red culotte under a knitted mesh robe, and the little yellow man with her has exchanged his checked suit for spotted swim trunks, his tattered valise for a red-yellow-green-and-white striped beach ball.

"We're off to the shore!" Mother-in-Law chirps; her beau grins just enough to reveal his sparsely toothed bottom gum.

"Well isn't that lovely," I say; but John turns his face away without saying a word. A petulant silence settles in the hallway as we all try to stare at each other, without appearing to look.

The stillness seems to remind Mother-in-Law of something; in a snap she unlocks her door and darts inside. She emerges with one of her familiar parcels, wrapped in old newspaper this time and tied with a dirty string.

"John, honey, this is for you," she coos. "I hope it fits!"

John takes the package but still averts his eyes.

Mother-in-Law

The trajectory of his glance seems to take in nothing but the stairwell, the fluorescent light, and the wilting potted plant by the mailboxes.

"Well, g'bye!" Mother-in-Law sings out; she takes her beau by the elbow, and with a rustle of plastic and wrinkled skin, they disappear out the door.

"I hate that man," John says, pouting and tugging at the string on his package.

"You!" I snap. "All you do is complain. At least *you* got a present!"

He hugs the package against his stomach as if he thinks I might take it from him; and in fact, that is just what I long to do. But instead I curl my claws against my palms, and we go back upstairs *(forgetting completely our reasons for coming down in the first place—that is the effect Mother-in-Law has on us—at the sight of her all of our plans are forgotten, suspended; awaiting, in some strange way, permission that she never seems to give).* We lay the package carefully on the kitchen table, and spend a great deal of time selecting the right knife to slit the string. The knife must not be too large; too large seems too threatening, too hostile, as if it were Mother-in-Law herself we'd be slicing. Then again too small seems disrespectful, as if the cord holding the package shut were unworthy of serious cutting. At last I select a pair of cooking shears and sever the string. Inside the package, my husband finds a white knit shirt and a little pair of blue knit swim trunks.

He holds them up doubtfully.

"Shall I try them on?"

"Sure," I say, "if you can get a leg into them."

For the swim trunks look absurdly small; and the white shirt likewise. It is long sleeved, with little pink ruffles at the cuffs.

Pouting, John disappears into the bedroom to try on the newest gifts. I wait in the kitchen. I make it my business to fold up the discarded news-wrap; I fold it into big squares, then smaller squares, then smaller squares, then smaller squares, until I can almost fit it under my fingernail.

John emerges wearing the little blue swim trunks.

"They fit!" I say, amazed.

"Just watch this," John says. He ducks back into the bedroom, and comes out dressed to the nines in his new white knit shirt. "It fits too," he says.

We stand for a moment in dumbfounded silence; how, I wonder, could the swimsuit look so small and still fit? And the shirt—what about that? The sleeves looked short, but now the pink cuff ruffles hang just where they're supposed to, straight from my husband's wrist to the first knuckle of his middle finger.

"There's no denying it," I say. "Love has done

your mother good. In the sense," I add hastily, not wanting to offend, "that she seems to be measuring much better."

"Yeah," John says, giving a little snort of laughter, "or maybe I'm shrinking."

We both laugh at that; then I pour us two vodkas and we speculate on the meaning of the latest gift. John thinks that the swim trunks are a good sign; maybe the next time his mother goes to the beach, she'll invite us to join her. I'm less certain.

"Maybe," I suggest, "this is her way of telling us to go to the beach ourselves. Sort of like, 'I've done my part, now you kids do the rest.'"

After several more vodkas, John realizes that this may be true. We go outside, hand in hand, to look for the quetzal among the branches of nearby evergreens.

In the morning, he is proved right: Mother-in-Law has slipped a note under our door. "Going to the shore with Henry tomorrow," the note reads. "Love to have you join us. 8 A.M. sharp!" The note is scrawled on what looks like a torn-off corner of newsprint; there's a greyness to it, and in one corner, something that looks like the edge of an underwear advertisement. Nonetheless, her handwriting is deep blue, compelling, and perhaps, we think, slightly perfumed. Underneath the creases of the underpants ad she's written a shaky P.S. "Wear your new trunks!"

It's easy to imagine Mother-in-Law saying this: her voice, we know, would be as clear as a quetzal's mating cry at morning. There is no question that we will go; that we must go; the note leaves no room for doubt. "8 A.M. sharp!"

The note gives rise to a flurry of arrangements. My husband must take the day off from work. There are towels to be folded, a cooler to be packed, lotions to be lined up, sniffed, and either tossed aside or packed among our other beach paraphernalia: several books *(Seashells of the Northern Shores* for me; for John an old favorite, *The Boy's Own Book of Detection,* along with his well-worn *Principles of Editorial Accounting);* sunglasses; decks of cards; paper and pens; and last but not least, a plastic bucket decorated with a series of images, white on red, of, in this order: a seashell (probably of the family *Melongenidae,* or common whelk), a starfish, a beach ball, a seagull, and a fish.

All day we have no time for the cry of the quetzal, the touching of hands, or the consideration of problems in the classification of the heart cockle. We pack our things, sip our wine, and anxiously contemplate the morning to come. I feel a familiar, ancient anticipation; like a child, I imagine that the softness of the bed sheets under my bare toes mimics the softness of the sand. For John the anticipation is different; it sounds like the hollow thud of a helium balloon bouncing against a white ceiling.

First thing in the morning, we're waiting outside Mother-in-Law's door, eagerly clutching our beach bags. For an hour we sit on the stairs, yawning and rubbing our eyes; then, finally, the door opens, and Mother-in-Law comes out, clad in a sheer pink nightie and fluffy slippers. *(Her hair sticks out in all directions, it's plain she's just gotten out of bed, but just the same I can't help but notice how good Mother-in-Law is looking—at first it seems undefinable, a sort of glow ["Mother-in-Law is in love," I think], but then the impression solidifies; I realize that she's no longer wiping at her filmy eye, that in fact the eye is no longer filmy. Both of Mother-in-Law's eyes are bright clear blue, and she's gaining weight—so much weight that I'd even, if pressed, say she was getting fat. But it's not an unhealthy, paunchy, saggy, old woman's fatness; it's a healthy fatness, a robustness, a fatness that is, if anything, redolent of life.)*

She blinks at us in surprise. "What are you kids up to?" she wonders.

John looks away, injured; so it is up to me to say it:

"The beach. Your note. That was today, wasn't it, Mother?"

Mother-in-Law clutches a salmon-colored hand to

her mouth. "Oh dear! I'm so embarrassed! You know, I'd completely forgotten! That happens a lot at the stage I'm at, you know!" She winks at me, and for a moment her hand rests on her protruding belly. Then she turns from the door. "Henry!" she bellows. "Out of bed, old man! We promised these kids a trip to the shore, and they're going to get it, by goodness!"

We hear Henry's sleepy groans, then the flush of running water; we catch a glimpse of the green interior; then Mother-in-Law pushes shut the door. For a last moment, her wide, flushed face peers around the corner at us.

"We'll be with you in a jiffy!" she says.

Then the door shuts, and we're left standing in the stairwell.

Another hour passes.

We hear sounds behind Mother-in-Law's door: laughter, clattering forks, slamming doors, furniture scraping across the floor, the blare of the television. John sits on the stairs, fingering his *Principles of Editorial Accounting*. There's a banging sound behind the door, as if someone is hammering.

"I think we should knock," John says.

I disagree.

"They might have forgotten us again."

"Well," I say, slowly, deliberately, calculatedly, "then, the hell with them!"

Mother-in-Law

My husband's face turns bright crimson. "That's *my mother* you're talking about!" He raises up his threatening *Principles of Editorial Accounting;* I reach defensively for *Seashells of the Northern Shores;* I'm about to make the preemptive strike when Mother-in-Law and her beau emerge, stepping smartly in their beachwear.

"Children!" Mother-in-Law scolds. "What are you doing? Put those books down! Now, c'mon, let's go!"

We sheepishly stash our books back in our beach bags, and trot out into the searing parking lot behind Mother-in-Law (her mesh knit beach robe is tied around her protruding belly with a wide red sash that flies out behind her in the breeze, tickling our noses) and Henry. Although we climb into John's car, Henry is behind the wheel. He wears a broad-brimmed Panama hat that hides his face; from the back, where we sit, all we can see is the cigarette that dangles coyly from his sagging lips, and the hairy corner of his right ear. Mother-in-Law shoves a cooler, the beach ball, a small suitcase, four blankets, an umbrella, four folding beach chairs, and a fabric bag (stuffed with smooth, clacking stuff that feels like clams) in the back with us.

"Makeup!" she explains, gaily, hopping into the front seat with Henry.

We drive to the shore. In the front seat, Mother-in-Law and Henry begin a round of song. I sit with one foot propped up on the cooler, the other tucked beneath me. John's head thuds against the ceiling every time Henry hits a bump.

We pass lawn ornaments, memorial markers, farm stands, county fairs, hair salons, hardware stores, political protests, cows, a cranberry bog, twenty-five gift shops, and a Dairy Queen.

"Are we there yet?" John asks.

"Very nearly, dear," Mother-in-Law says.

We pass a library. A drug store. A church. An art gallery. Maple trees (at least eighty). Pine trees (at least seventy-five). A statue of Columbus. A seat of government. A park bench (occupied). Two park benches (unoccupied). A beauty contest. A sheltie, straining at the leash. An elegant birch. A lost glove. An orange-roofed Tast-EE-Freeze.

"Are we there yet?" I ask.

I don't say so, but my foot is getting cold.

In the front seat, Mother-in-Law is humming something about bottles, a wall, passing 'em around, etc.

"No, dear," she says absentmindedly. "Soon."

I look at John, but he only smiles pacifically. His head no longer butts against the ceiling.

"You're shrinking," I say. I say it to be cruel, but just for a split second, it seems to be true.

John smiles at me. "Yes," he says, drawing out each letter very, very slowly.

We begin to laugh. Mother-in-Law and Henry begin to laugh, too, in the front seat. We round a corner, and the ocean comes into view. It's a strip of blue, nestled tight beneath the chin of the blue sky.

"See," said Mother-in-Law, "I told you we were almost there!"

We pull into a parking lot littered with empty things: bags of chips, greasy boxes of popcorn, hot dog wrappers, shattered clam shells. There's a scene as we unload the car: Mother-in-Law is too big to lift herself out of the front seat; John, trapped behind her, wails to get out. As for me, I'm blocked by the cooler, the beach ball, a small suitcase, four blankets, an umbrella, four folding beach chairs, and a fabric bag stuffed with makeup. Only Henry can get free, and he takes his time: he stretches, yawns, and leans against the car, finishing a smoke.

"Henry! Henry! Help me get out of this thing!" Mother-in-Law shouts. Henry drops his butt onto the pavement and carefully grinds it out with his sandal. Then he strolls around to the other side of the car.

As for me, I decide to take action: I pick up the makeup bag and throw it out of the car. I hear the tinkle of a dozen mirrors shattering as the bag hits the pavement. The beach chairs are next; I thrust those out the door as well. The suitcase is easy—one kick and it's in the parking lot. Although I don't look, I can hear Henry panting and groaning as he tries to extract Mother-in-Law from the front seat.

"Good Lord, Maude, you're getting bigger every day!" Henry exclaims. "Maybe if I turn you this way . . ."

Mother-in-Law giggles, there's a cheerful popping sound, like a cork coming out of a champagne bottle, and she lands on her rump by the side of the car. John spills out on top of her. Suddenly, I feel foolish. I step out of the car into a pile of beach paraphernalia. "What a mess!" I say, showing my teeth to good advantage.

Laden with all of our stuff (I carry the chairs, the blankets, the suitcase and the umbrella; Henry has the cooler; Mother-in-Law holds the beach ball upon her bulging tummy; and as for John, his arms are too short to carry anything but the fabric bag, filled now with a jingling cacophony of plastic compacts split open like clamshells), we finally turn toward the ocean. We hear the rush and suck of the waves; hot sand shifts and shimmers beneath our sandaled feet.

"This way!" says Mother-in-Law, pointing toward an unoccupied spit of sand (for the sand is occupied—everywhere we look, although we try not to see them, beach umbrellas spring up around us like multicolored mushrooms; pungent screams emanating beneath these fabric fungi warn us of infants underfoot; portable radios compete with the seagulls; buttocks smeared with coconut oil thrust themselves before our eyes; John steps, accidentally, upon someone's bologna sandwich. Cries of protest rise from the sands).

"I love to see the sea!" Mother-in-Law sings; her voice cuts through the beach din like the chime of a bell. She points her nose skyward and takes great big snuffs of the salt air. "This is just the spot!" She drops the beach ball onto the sand, and then herself.

Henry and I scurry to unroll the blankets and unfurl the umbrella. As soon as she's shifted onto her blanket, Mother-in-Law produces a ball of blue yarn and begins to knit. John disappears down the beach with his red and white bucket. Mother-in-Law looks after him, and sighs.

"He's become such a fine boy! Don't those new trunks look lovely on him?"

A seagull coughs in reply.

We all lie on our blankets, there in a row before the seagreen sea. Henry dexterously lights a new cigarette from the shrinking butt of the old; Mother-in-Law clicks her needles; I languorously turn the pages of *Seashells of the Northern Shores*. I can see John, far down the beach, stooping over a hole in the sand. It's not an uncomfortable silence, but I feel compelled to offer a comment, just the same.

"John's smaller than he used to be," I say.

Henry aims a smoke ring around the head of a nearby gull. Mother-in-Law clicks.

"Not that I'm complaining," I say.

Mother-in-Law smiles and nods.

"There are advantages. His new clothes fit him better. But just the same," I say, "it's odd. Don't you think so, Mother?"

She finally glances up from her knitting, with the provoked look of an enraged warthog.

"My John is becoming a fine boy," she snaps, "and I won't hear *you* say otherwise, Missy!"

(I imagine her in the underbrush, tangled in a net of yarn, rolling over rocks and scrub and anthills, rolling toward the fertile plains, rolling toward the distant Himalaya, trying to escape my fateful jaw . . .)

"Yes, Mother," I say.

Henry makes a sound like chuckling.

We all turn over on our blankets.

"There's something so melodious about the sound of the sea!" Mother-in-Law says, and sighs. She clicks in unison with the waves; she might be knitting an ocean: click—*swoosh!* click—*swoosh!* click—*swoosh!* I lie on my blanket with my nose toward the sand, and imagine dark things scuttling beneath the

water: crabs in silt, a green-eyed lobster, the silky
sweet breath of the sole. And others, too: the steamy
bivalve, the patient mollusk; lives on the shell or the
half-shell. What could the oysters be thinking? Is
there a quetzal, under the sea?

Click and *swoosh* subside, and I fall into an aque-
ous dream in which Mother-in-Law recedes before
me through caverns of coral and bone. She's got spiny
red fins, a laughing face, two big spots of rouge on
her cheeks. We dart in tandem through leafy fronds,
pirouette above the sea stars, suck diaphanous baby
shrimp out of the sand. No matter how I try to catch
up, Mother-in-Law is always just ahead of me, wink-
ing at me with her big, flat, straw-colored eyes (amazing how eyes so big, so flat, so straw-colored, can be
at the same time so expressive, so loving). Even as
she sucks up the shrimp, the mussels, the diatoms,
the coral polyps, the anchovies, the sea worms and
sea jellies, the luxuriant sponges, the twirling anemo-
nes, the water fleas, and hydras and volvox and lan-
goustines, those big, flat, golden, loving eyes seem
to say: "Don't worry, dear. There's plenty for both
of us!"

And then she disappears. There's a rock erupting
with barnacles; I stop for a moment to probe there
with my slender tongue; I look up, and she's gone.

I'm terrified, alone in the watery dark. I must find

my Mother-in-Law! I race past black weaving fingers of seaweed, in and out of sea caves where snapping jaws lie waiting in patient obscurity, through cacophonous schools of tuna, over and up and around the pink spirals of coral, higher and higher until the water turns warm, translucent, and blue. But there is no Mother-in-Law; no Mother-in-Law anywhere at all.

I give up. I sink. I'm alone, completely alone, in the vast cold sea.

Then all at once I'm in the changing room of my favorite department store, trying on bathing suits. Mother-in-Law is with me! She's there, just outside the curtain! She's handing me bathing suits, one after another.

"Try this one, dear!"

I try. I try. I try. But Mother, they're too small! They're children's bathing suits, Mother-in-Law!

"Nonsense, dear. Why, that looks lovely! Come on out here and model!"

Miserably, I try to tug the suit down. I'm half naked! But she wants me to model! There's a slight smell of cigarette smoke, a glimpse of a hairy ear— *Henry, waiting outside the curtain!*

I won't do it! I won't!

I wake up, gasping, with my face in the sand. There's a periwinkle stuck to my thumbnail; one of

Henry's cigarette butts lies perilously close to my ear. I think: Something's different. Something's changed. I roll over and see that the beach is empty; the scarlet sun is languorously melting into the sea.

I'm mumbling something. What?

"I must have slept for hours," I say, my tongue thick with the gritty effluvia of the tides.

Mother-in-Law is talking to someone. "Okay, dear, now turn around and let me check the back," she's saying. "Good! Good! That looks very nice!"

I sit up, and see Mother-in-Law pinning a little blue jersey on a sunburned, scrawny, blond-headed boy.

I have to admit it: I'm touched.

"That's very sweet of you, Mother-in-Law," I say.

Mother-in-Law looks young and happy in the evening light. She smiles at me. "He's a fine boy," she says.

I wish she'd knit something for me.

Henry scratches at the crotch of his blue and yellow trunks and says he wants to leave. The blond boy exclaims with disappointment. I think: What a charming child. Friendly.

"I guess it's about that time," Mother-in-Law says. "It's been a lovely day. Hasn't it been a lovely day?"

Yes, we all agree, it's been a lovely day. Henry tugs Mother-in-Law to her feet; then he and I pack up the beach things. We head for the car.

"Wait!" I say, suddenly aware of an empty space at my side. "Where's John? We can't leave without John!"

They all begin to laugh at me: Mother-in-Law, Henry, and the little boy. The seagulls are laughing, the sea grass, the sand dunes, even the rocks (usually, so impassive). The boy pulls playfully at my stack of towels.

"Here I am, silly!" he says, giggling and sticking his pink tongue through a gap in his teeth. "I'm right here!"

"Of course he's here," Mother-in-Law says. "I wouldn't leave my very own boy, would I?"

They all agree she wouldn't, and we climb into the car.

There are advantages, I suppose. A smaller John takes up less space in the back seat, but he bounces more and makes weird sounds. Mother-in-Law leans over and cleans the sand off his face with her own saliva.

"Can't move around much with this big belly!" she chuckles.

We chuckle sympathetically.

That night I return to my apartment alone. I lie

alone in my big bed, listening for the cry of the quetzal. I can hear all kinds of noises from downstairs: the television blaring, dishes clattering, the hollow ringing thuds of a ball bouncing against the ceiling, the clattering footsteps of a child. Smoke from Henry's cigarette floats in my bedroom window.

It's a lonely feeling.

In the morning I go downstairs; I tell Mother-in-Law, very somberly, that I want to take John to breakfast. This way, I think, he and I will have a chance to talk about it all—maybe I can counteract Mother-in-Law; maybe, somehow, I can cajole him into growing up again.

But once we get to the restaurant, I can't get him to talk to me at all. He's wearing one of his mother's little knit outfits (I notice, with a thrill of despair, that even now *the sleeves are too short*). He orders chocolate milk. He's got a little tin car that he rolls up and down my arms. It's annoying.

I think how glad I am that we never had children.

After a few hours I feel compelled to take him back to his mother. I've never been much of one for baby-sitting. Children have always bothered me: so much noise, drooling, puddles of mess; their smell, like tarnished nickels.

And so John disappears into his mother's apartment; I let him disappear. I see a narrow glimpse of the interior forest; the door shuts in my face; our life together is over.

But of course, I still have my binoculars. I see them together: Mother-in-Law, Henry, and John, heading across the parking lot to their car, laden with beach things or picnic baskets or baseballs and bats. They look so happy, singing and swinging their hampers of cold chicken and potato salad. Sometimes it seems to me that John looks younger than before; Mother-in-Law looks wider; but I squint, I rub my eyes, and the illusion disappears. One day I'm at the aquarium (slowly, reluctantly, I've once again taken up the habits of the single life: visits to the aquarium, the botanical gardens, the art museum, even, at moments of lonely desperation, the heliocopter museum of our fine city); I round a corner past the bubbling octopi; and I see Mother-in-Law in front of me. Suddenly I'm overtaken by the frenzy of my dream. I long to speak to her.

I call out, "Mother! Mother-in-Law!"

She turns and sees me. Then she runs.

I think she's holding something. I think she's got a baby in her arms.

After that day I don't see them any more: neither Mother-in-Law nor Henry nor John. I still hear noises from downstairs, but even those are muted, as if they didn't want me to hear. Once or twice, I think there's a baby crying, but it's hard to tell. The sound rises quickly and is just as suddenly muted—it could have been the wind, or my quetzal.

Finally I surprise her. I rise very early, and sneak downstairs and out, and there's Mother-in-Law, working in her garden. She's wearing a big gauzy red dress and she's on her knees in the dirt; I see the brown bottoms of her feet. She's let her hair grow. It's long and blond and tumbles around her face; I can't see her face at all.

"Mother!" I say.

She turns around. She turns. It's Mother-in-Law, but she's very young. She's like a picture from John's photo album. She blinks at me, pushes the golden hair out of her face; finally, she stands, and I can see that she's pregnant: hugely pregnant, irremediably pregnant, undeniably *with child*.

She's younger than I am.

"Yes, dear?"

But I have nothing to say to her. I smile, and go back inside.

And now I'm packing. I'm taking everything: my sea-shells and gemstones and stuffed birds and butter-flies, my pressed flowers, even the teeth. And my bin-oculars; I'll wear those; I'll hang them around my neck as I run. I can leave the less important stuff, like furniture and clothes. It's imperative that I leave. This morning, leaning on the windowsill, I saw something that convinced me: my own mother, walking up the walk, carrying her suitcases and her birdcage; my own mother, shaking Mother-in-Law by the hand, looking as if she intended to stay.